WDCRN

The Hollow Land

JANE GARDAM

THE HOLLOW LAND

illustrated by Janet Rawlins

Greenwillow Books
New York

Library of Congress
Cataloging in Publication Data
Gardam, Jane.   The hollow land.
Summary: Young Harry Bateman comes
from London with his family year after
year to spend the summer at Light Trees
Farm in the Cumbrian fell country,
until he feels that it is his real home.
[1. Farm life—England—Fiction.
2. England—Fiction]
I. Rawlins, Janet, ill.   II. Title.
PZ7.G163Ho   [Fic]   81-6620
ISBN 0-688-00873-9   AACR2

For Tom Gardam
and in memory of his friend,
old Tom Richardson

Contents

Christ keep the Hollow Land
Through the sweet spring-tide
When the apple blossoms bless
The lowly bent hill side.

Christ keep the Hollow Land
All the summer-tide.
Still we cannot understand
Where the waters glide.

Only dimly seeing them
Coldly slipping through
Many green-lipp'd cavern mouths,
Where the hills are blue.

William Morris

1 · Bell and Harry

I'm Bell Teesdale. I'm a lad. I'm eight.

All down this dale where I live there's dozens of little houses with grass growing between the stones and for years there's been none of them wanted. They're too old or too far out or that bit too high for farmers now. There was miners once – it's what's called the hollow land – but they're here no more. So the little houses is all forsook.

They have big garths round them, and pasture for grass-letting – sheep and that – and grand hay fields. Maybe just too many buttercups blowing silver in June, but grand hay for all that, given a fair week or two after dipping time.

All these little farm houses for years stood empty, all the old farming families gone and the roofs falling in and the swallows and swifts swooping into bedrooms and muck trailing down inside the stone walls.

So incomers come. They buy these little houses when they

9

can, or they rent or lease them. Manchester folks or even London folks, with big estate cars full of packet food you don't see round here, and great soft dogs that's never seen another animal.

All down Mallerstang there's becks running down off the fell. It's bonny. Down off the sharp scales, dry in summer till one single drop of rain sends them running and rushing and tumbling down the fell-side like threads of silk. Like cobwebs. And when the wind blows across the dale these becks gasp, and they rise up on theirselves like the wild horses in Wateryat Bottom. They rise up on their hind legs. Or like smoke blowing, like ever so many bonfires, not water at all, all smoking in the wind between Castledale and the Moorcock toward Wensleydale. It's bonny.

And townsfolk come looking at all this now where once they only went to the Lake District over the west. Renting and leasing they come. Talking south. "Why'd they come?" I ask our grandad who's leased the farm house he used to live in (my gran died). "There's not owt for 'em here. What's use of a farm to them? Just for sitting in. Never a thing going on."

"Resting," says my grandad. "They take 'em for resting in after London."

Well, this family that come to my grandad's old house, Light Trees, wasn't resting. Not resting at all. There's a mother and a father and four or five great lads, some of them friends only, and there's a little lad, Harry, and the racket they make can be heard as far as Garsdale likely.

They has the house – our gran and grandad's old house, see – but we still keep all the farm buildings and work them and we've right to the hay off the Home Field. There's good cow byres, dipping pens, bull's hull and clipping shed. So we're clipping and dipping and drenching and putting the cows to the bull regardless. Sometimes there's a hundred sheep solid across our yard so they can't get their car over to the yard gate. But it was in the arrangement, mind. My dad always says, "We're about to bring in sheep, Mr Bateman" – it's what they're called, Bateman – "We're bringing in sheep. Would you like to get your car out first? We'll hold things back." There's maybe four, five and six of our sheep-dogs lying watching, and their soft dog lying watching our dogs, but never going near. Then from out the house comes their music playing, and lads yelling and laughing and a radio or two going and the London mother cooking these Italian-style suppers and their telephone ringing (they've got in the telephone like they've got in a fridge) and they're all saying, this London lot, *"Beautiful* evening Mr Teesdale" – my dad – "and what are you doing with the sheep tonight? You're giving us quite an edu*cation*."

And there's this little lad, Harry, just stands there not saying owt.

Now there's one night, the first night of hay-time, and we're all slathered out, even my dad. It's perfect. A right hot summer and a right hot night and a bright moon. Yesterday my dad said, "Tomorrow we'll mow hay. We'll mow all day and if need be through the night. There may be rain by Sunday."

He's never wrong, my dad, so we – my mum and our Eileen and our Eileen's boyfriend and Grandad and all of us – we set up till we'd mowed and we finish the High Field and Miner's Acre by tea-time. And then we sets to with the Home Field – that's the great big good field round Light Trees. Light Trees stands right in it.

It makes a rare clatter our tractor and cutter, louder than their transistors – clatter, clatter, clatter, round and round and round – and after a bit, well maybe two hours, there's heads beginning to bob from windows. Then round ten-eleven o'clock and the summer light starts fading and it's still clatter, clatter, there's electric lights flashing on and off inside Light Trees and this London father comes out.

11

First he just stands there. Then he strolls and watches. Clatter, clatter, clatter. Round and round and round. He starts waving a bit. Then he's calling. Finally, round midnight he's yelling and shouting at us, but we can't stop. When you open up a field of hay you have to see it mowed out.

And then the tractor breaks down and there's silence. Silence like the beginning of the world or the end of it, and the London father and some of the big lads comes over (the mother's inside with ear-plugs in likely, the cutter coming up to the house wall, see, every two-three minutes, though not *that* near. Further off as we get nearer the middle) and he says, "Will this row be going on much longer then, Teesdale?"

"Not if I can get this feller mended," says my dad, fratcheting with spanners.

"Causing something of a row," says the London father.

"No row here," says my dad, "*I'm* having no row."

"No, no," says the London father, "*making* a row. You're making one devil of a row."

"None of my making," says my dad, pushing his jaw forward and getting aloft the tractor again and the racket starts up even louder than ever, blue smoke rising from the tractor chimney in the moonlight.

They'd got at cross purposes, see. First meaning of row with us seems to be quarrel. First meaning of row with them seems to mean noise, or at any rate it does tonight. I could see this, but my dad was busy, and tired, and working ahead of rain, so he took no heed. My dad might have been talking Chinese for all the London man tried to understand him and the London man might have been talking Eskimo. The big lads looked soft about it, too, and started muttering and kicking their feet about in the new short grass left by the cutter. "Country peace and quiet," says one. "Country peace and *quaat*. Worse than Piccadilly Circus."

Bell and Harry

I stood back like. I'd been sent to the clipping shed for more John Robert before I went to check the fell gate was shut for the night, and as I crosses the field back I sees this little lad, Harry, looking out of his bedroom window and I catches his eye. And somehow I know he's all right, this one, London boy or not. I know he understands how we have to make all this racket to see hay cut ahead of rain. Maybe all night long we have to go on. With lights fixed up, even. I give him a bit wave, and he disappears his head out of sight. Dips it down shy-like. You'd not think of London folk being shy.

So, well by morning, we're finished. And next day we strow and turn. And very next day after – it being such a wonderful hot summer – we begin to bale and elevate into barns, doing the Light Trees' Home Field first for their convenience to get it over for them. A rare noisy job of course it is and the London folks all walked away out of it – the whole band of them! Going off across the yard in boots, and packs on their backs for an all-day hike. But by the Saturday night we're off the fell. We're back down in our own farm kitchen, down the village, all fields finished and very satisfied. We're all over aching. We're slow speaking. We've done with moving for a week. With hay-time for another year. My dad says, "I'm away. Bed for me," and then as he gets his hand on the knob at the end of our old staircase he says, "You shut yon fell gate now, Bell?"

I said I had.

"You're sure now?"

"Aye, I'm sure."

"Well, I'm away."

And I starts to wonder. Every single night since my gran died and grandad moved down here with us and my dad began to farm the Light Trees land he's checked this fell gate. It's a long old gate in the last stone wall before the open fell. It's on a path that walkers use. They walk in clumps –

great fat orange folk with long red noses and maps in plastic cases flapping across their stomachs. Transistors going sometimes too and looking at nowt before them but their own two feet. Sometimes the walkers up front leave the gates open for the straggling ones coming behind. Then the stragglers think that's how the gate's meant to be, and leave it. Then the cows come out of the pasture and on to the fell and the sheep come off the fell and in to the pasture and on and away till they're mixed in with other folks's sheep and cows where maybe there's a ram and certainly a bull. And then there's merry hell. "Better to check that gate every night of our lives," says my dad, "than rue it."

Lately – since I grew to be eight – checking the gate's been my job. Well, up I goes to bed – and I wonder.

Did I shut it?

I gets out of my clothes and I rolls in to my bed and it's grand and soft. I wriggle about in to the shape of me in the middle of the springs – if you filled it up with candle grease and let it cool and lifted the candle grease out you'd have a statue of me sleeping. The moon's shining in at the window and I'm dead beat and I'm all over scratched with hay. My eyes is dropping and every muscle of me is like stones.

Did I then?

Shut that fell gate?

He'd be in a fair taking if –

So out I gets and in to my clothes again and down the stairs. Great roaring snores. My mum and dad sleep that sound after hay-time they often sleep right through the alarm clock stood by the bedside in a bucket. Away I went, off up the road the two miles up to Light Trees and the half mile beyond it to the fell gate.

He were wrong, Dad, for once. It's midnight so it's Sunday. "There'll be rain by Sunday," he said – and there's no rain. The moon's as huge and bright as the past three nights and the fells laid out all colours beneath it. There's rabbits here and rabbits there and cows lumbering up on to their knees as they hear you coming, rolling their eyes and crashing off in to the shadows of the little black may trees. And there's my own three Leicester ewes glaring at me out of green lamp eyes, faces like camels, right snooty. And there's curlews that calls out to each other all night long, just like in the day, and never seems to sleep. And there's no sound else up here but the becks running.

There's no sign of life as I pass Light Trees. Tired out with walking they've been keeping to theirselves, the London folk, nobody speaking. They crossed the yard twice today while we were there, not speaking. It's tight lips and heads turned sideways.

"Likely they're going to tek off," my grandad said this afternoon.

"Not without paying their rent they won't," says my dad. "I'd say they'd rested theirselves enough anyway."

"It is their holidays," said our Eileen who likes the looks of the big London lads, though she won't let on. "It's a shame for them really. It's spoiling their summer. They'd wanted to come back and back for five years at least. And all that money they've spent on telephones and that."

"Well they don't have to go," says Dad. "All's quiet for them now. Hay-time's over. They can play their radios full tilt in peace."

"They'll go and they'll never come back," wails Eileen.

"Others'll come," says my dad. "There's any amount of incomers without farm houses to go round for them now. But they'll have to learn our ways. Standing there rowing in fields!"

My grandad says that hay-time's maybe not understood by them as important and maybe there's things of theirs we don't catch on to either.

I say, "And he weren't rowing, the London father, not *rowing*," and my dad says, "You keep quiet."

I'm up at the fell gate by now – and what d'you think? It's open! Stood right back on itself and wide open and even the John Robert gone that binds it. It's just what he said'd happen one day and never has. I stand there feeling that grand that I bothered to come out and see. No signs of stock straying yet, thanks be. But many more thanks be that I bothered to come.

I shut the gate, but it's still not fast without binding and there's plenty of John Robert down in Light Trees clipping shed, so off I go, taking the short cut down the slope of Hartley Birket and over the wall and through the Home Field with Light Trees standing in the middle of it. The field looks smooth now with the hay got in – light as my head when my grandad's clipped the hair off it. Hay-time done, grand hot summer ahead, my shadow twelve foot long from the moon. I feel quite drunk and cheerful.

They'd get some fright if they looked out and saw me now, this London lot, thinks I. Ghosts and vampires, thinks I, and begins to flap my arms about. I'm right up now against the back wall of Light Trees and I'm looking right in at the little back bedroom window (the house being dug down snug in the side of the fell, upstairs at the back having its chin on the grass so to speak) and I feel like gawping in the window and making whoo-whoo noises, scaring the moonlights out of the soppy lot.

But coming up to the window I sees it's open and there's the little lad, Harry, standing there looking out. Standing quite still. And it's way after midnight.

I near passed out cold. I just stood there.

Yet he weren't afraid a bit.

He must have seen me vampiring away from miles off. And he's not afraid a bit.

After a bit longer I see he's crying.

He's just a little lad see – maybe four or five. Maybe six.

I think maybe, though he don't look frightened, he's

16

crying *with* fright, so to speak, and I say – when I get a bit of strength back – I sort of whispers it, thinking of that little house behind him all brimful of people, great knowing London people – "It's only me. Bell Teesdale."

Sniff, he goes, sniff.

"I'm not doing owt," I say.

Sniff.

"I just been checking on the fell gate. It's been left open."

Sniff.

"I'm just coming on down here for the John Robert."

Sniff.

Sniff. Then, at last – "What's John Robert?"

"Well, string. Farmer's string. For combines and that. It's always been called that. You don't know a lot, do you?"

He starts crying again. "What's matter?" says I. "Don't get upset now."

"We're going home tomorrow. I don't want to go home."

"Why you going then?"

"My father says he won't be bossed by your father and there's too much noise. He works writing. He has to be quiet. Six weeks it was to be, our holiday here. All the school holidays."

"It's only once a year," I say. "We only cut once a year. Then it's quiet as owt. Except clipping time and dipping time and when lambs get taken from their mothers and there's a bit bleating, there's never a sound here. Not so much as a motor except once a day the postman."

He says, "My father says he can't do with fumes and smoke and racket. That's what he came to get away from."

"It's over till next year."

"We're still going, though," says Harry and starts to cry again. "My mother wrote a letter to your mother to say she was sorry if we'd given offence but my father wouldn't let her send it.

"I don't want to go home," he says. "It's just streets and

17

streets. Why didn't your father *say* hay-time was just once?"

"Likely he thought there was nobody in the world didn't know. He were clashed. Could you not see how my dad were clashed out? And the tractor broke. And expecting rain. Anyway – noise! What about all your radios and stereos and portable tellies?"

He can't think what to say to this so he begins to cry again. "Town yobs," says I.

He picks up something heavy – maybe a transistor. Not even our Eileen's got her own and she's seventeen, and I say, "Now think on. Hold still. Let's have a think. Where's your mother's letter?"

"Thrown away. In the bin under the sink."

"Crumpled up?"

"No – just thrown."

"Can you get it?"

"Well, I could."

"Get it," says I. "I'm going for the John Robert in the shed. I'll come back round this way and you can give it me."

When I come back he hands the letter over.

"D'you want to come out?" I say. "You can come up and fasten the fell gate with me if you want. Get some shoes on."

He's over the sill in his shoes and his jersey over his pyjamas in half a minute flat, and we go off doing silent vampires over the Home Field. At the beck we make a change to space men and while I'm fixing the fell gate we're the S.A.S. and have a bit of quiet machine-gunning. I see he gets back in through his window, for there's rain coming now, great cold plops at first, then armies like running mice, and the moon all suddenly gone. He takes a header in through his window from a standing start. He's not a bad 'un this Harry.

Then I'm away. Over the hill and down the road, past the quarry and under the bridge and in to the village and dripping wet through our own front door. I left it unlatched (great snores still going on above) and I put the letter from under my shirt down carefully in the middle of the doormat. It's a pity she hadn't had time to put it in an envelope. They look a family for envelopes. But we'll have to see.

Then I dried myself off a bit and slithered in to my bed and I didn't wake till long past milking.

When I got down they'd finished breakfast and my mum's been baking. Yawning but baking. Our Eileen's still in bed and not a sign of Grandad. "Grandad's seen plenty haytimes," says my dad, "but he's slower now forgetting them."

My mum's putting six or seven grand big tea-cakes in to a paper bag and my father's carrying eggs and some new milk in a can.

"What's yon?" says I.

"It's for them up at Light Trees," says my mum. "They get little enough in London fit to eat. They may as well get some benefit here."

I met up with the lad, Harry, later beyond the fell gate. He joined up with me behind Dad's tractor which was laden up with dead sheep getting a bit ripe and on their way to being dropped down a shackhole. It's right horrible putting dead sheep down shackholes. You wait ages till you hear them splash. Just think of falling in yourself! Harry loved it. Our four dogs was dancing all around him jumping up and licking his face.

"All's right then now?" I ask.

He says, "Seems like."

"You're stopping then? Not away off back to London?"

"We're stopping. There's been not another word."

"Nowt said?"

"No. Your dad just came walking in with buns."

"Tea-cakes."

"Tea-cakes. And milk and eggs."

"What did your mum say?"

"When he'd gone she said, 'This puts us to shame. I didn't even send that letter.'"

"I hope she doesn't see it's gone."

"She won't. She'd never think. She's not sensible."

"And that was all?"

"No. After that my father went across the yard to your father and they shook hands."

Harry and I walked on after – away over Green Fell Crag behind the tractor, squidging in the soaking turf. And every now and then there comes the rain like Dad said, and the clouds are fat and purple with the sun flashing in and out of them, and my dad singing on the tractor cock-a-hoop and loud as larks because he's done with hay-time before the rain and there's other folks all round not yet dared start.

I said, "Harry, you're going to settle here now. I just feel it. There's not many do. Not incomers to these old farms and different, like you lot are. But I'd say you'd settle for plenty holidays now."

And Harry said, "I've settled."

2 · The Egg Witch

Harry sat happily on Jamie the old horse rake that stood in the yard with the nettles sticking up high through its round, rusty ribs. He sang as he bounced in the curved iron saddle and clanked the gears and handles. Behind in Light Trees every door and window stood wide open and Harry's mother lay spread about on a sofa, dabbing her face against heat and looking out every two minutes anxiously across the yard at Harry.

Around the yard stood the square of fortifications of stone barns and sheep pens and above them, stretching far, far away were the fells, bright pink-yellow turning hazy with heat. Their horizon jigged like the desert. Not a sheep or a cow seemed to move, humped in under the stone walls, looking for shadow. No walkers passed to the Pennine Way. Not even the curlews were conversational.

The rest of the Batemans had taken themselves off climbing in the car. "Climbing in the car," sang Harry. They had gone to High Cup Nick, hoping for cool air. Harry's mother had stopped behind to mind him because Harry climbed – and walked too for that matter – rather zig-zag which meant he went double the distance at half the speed. She had also stopped behind to get some peace and quiet, for except for Harry her family were going through a noisy and argumentative time just now, wagging their fingers a lot at each other and shouting above the radios.

When the car had roared away over the ribbony white road and they had watched the cloud of dust at its heels die away after it had tipped over forwards down Quarry Hill, the silence settled like limestone dust. Harry's mother gave a thankful sigh, walked back in to Light Trees and fell on the sofa with a book, and Harry climbed upon Jamie and sang.

It was a drone perhaps rather than a song, and it went on and on. He droned at the nettles, at the invisible horse in the thin old dropped-down shafts of the rake which was still faintly painted blue. He droned at the dusty cherry trees hanging over the orchard wall. He droned at the pink fell and the track up it to the haunted tarn and the old mines and the bumpy lines on Hartley Birket which people said were ancient railways.

Harry was happy. But his mother was not. Edgy, fidgetty, she couldn't keep to her book. She looked at Harry once, twice. She wondered if there was something odd about him sitting there all by himself not wanting someone to play with.

So much younger than James, she thought. I oughtn't to be lying here. I ought to be off finding him a friend. He'll be getting shy and funny. It's not natural – droning on a horse rake.

Also it was Sunday which always meant scrambled eggs for supper and she had run out of eggs. She would have to go down to get eggs from Teesdales. Perhaps Bell Teesdale might ask Harry to stay down there and play.

So the two of them set off walking in the heat of the

afternoon, up the ribbony road and tipping over the hill as the car had done, past the great sleeping lime quarry dazzling the sky; on past the row of dusty fir trees all covered in grey powder; under the bridge where the bones of a young woman and the bones of her child had been discovered by quarrymen last year. They had been curled together in a sleeping position, the child inside the mother's arms for about four thousand years. You could tell their date by the way they lay curled. They were Beaker People. Harry's mother thought that she perhaps ought to be telling Harry about all this and especially about the dates because it would help with school.

But Harry was zig-zagging and droning ahead. He droned at the showers of blackberry bushes hanging over the road, pricking with pins, and at the dry beck with the little bridges down the village street. Looking down at the beck and the village was a farm called Castle Farm where a Great Lord of the Marches had lived more than three hundred years ago. He had loved the king and had ridden all the way from the fells to Westminster for a coronation. The jewels in his sword and harness and on his clothes had cost so much that he had no money afterwards and someone wrote it all down in a book. Harry's mother knew all about it. She wanted to tell Harry. But Harry was too interested in the peeling paint on the rail of the little bridge and the ducks complaining of the lack of water in the beck. She wondered if it had been a dry day or a wet one when the Lord of the Marches had crossed the beck on his way to Westminster Abbey.

In the middle of the village street Flora the fluffy dog lay curled in a shallow pot-hole fast asleep. No quarry lorries came by on a Sunday and so Flora felt safe. She knew Sundays like a Christian. Four tired, hot hens jerked russet necks out of a hedge and made long complaining sounds in their throats and bobbed back in again. Not a soul stirred down the village street.

When Harry's mother knocked on Teesdales' front door –

the farm house was close on the road – there was no reply and – a wonder – the door was locked. All Mrs Teesdale's lupins in the narrow front garden, pink and pale yellow and purple and lavender blue and deep rich glowing red like the Lord of the Marches' rubies, stood there looking at Harry and his mother and saying clearly,

"Did you forget then? They've all gone off to Morecambe to the sea. Even old Grandad Hewitson."

"They're all at the sea," said a voice from a dark place. Harry's mother turned to see Flora's master, Jimmie Metcalf (called Meccer), shadowy in the back of his tottery dark shed by the road side. He had been lamed in the quarry long since and could work no more, but he kept in touch by sitting in the shed and watching the limestone go by in great white lumps on the lorries, and on Sundays watching his dog sleep in the limestone lane. He was a huge fat pale man with a large flat face and straight-ahead eyes. He knew every mortal thing you did, Mrs Teesdale said, even before you had done it. Now he said to Harry's mother, "Your eggs will be round the dairy at the back. It'll not be locked."

"Oh that I *couldn't* do," said Mrs Bateman, "not without asking."

"No shops open," said the voice from the dark of the shed.

"We have some tins," said Mrs Bateman, not very proudly.

"There'll be eggs further along," said Flora's master. "They sells eggs along at Blue Barns. It's straight down the lanes. It's barely a step."

So Harry's mother called to where Harry was lying in the middle of the road stroking Flora whose eyes were tight shut as usual, and they went on down the village and in to Jingling Lane, then up and round a cluster of farms and a pub and on to Gypsies' Hill.

Gypsies' Hill was interesting because it had a big post on it with a notice saying GYPSIES PROHIBITED. The council repainted it every year or two. Yet every year the gypsies came and settled in round the post and hung a line of washing from it. Maybe six or seven times a year they would suddenly be there with their huge caravans you'd never think could get down the lane and their filthy tin cans and children and heaps of rubbish and a pony or two tied up and a fire going. Then just as suddenly they'd be gone.

Today they were here. In force. Very comfortable. The fire burned bright making the hot day shimmer. The washing was hanging on the line and they were all sitting about doing nothing at all like Jimmie Meccer. But they were more separate. Harry's mother felt uneasy with gypsies and her heart beat faster as she went by the hot, still place.

But a man smiled at her and she said, "Good afternoon." "Good day my lovely," said a brown young woman to Harry and Harry said hello and waved.

On they went down a lane so narrow that the bushes tangled their fingers together overhead. The ruts under their feet were sharp and crumbly and stars of flowers shone in the high banks – campion and speedwell and yellow and purple vetches and plumy grasses and little brown-pink orchidy things and long arches of flimsy wild roses.

They came out of this lane to a place where three lanes meet and took the one sign-posted to Blue Barns.

"Blue Barns is a pretty name," said Harry's mother still dazzled by the flowers she had picked and the sudden sunlight as they came out in to the open. Harry lifted his arms and began to drone and be an aeroplane.

"Oh stop that silly singing," said his mother. "Can't you *talk* to me?" Harry stopped singing – he was always good – and came back and took his mother's hand though he didn't talk to her.

So they came to Blue Barns which was painted black. Every bit of it that could be painted was painted black –

black barns, black byres, black window frames, hulls, chicken houses, sheds, front gate, back gate, dog kennel and even the front door. Black is a bad colour against Cumbrian stone and scarcely ever seen. On the front gate was painted in white BLUE BARNS.

Every window and door was tight shut. The yard looked scrubbed without a wisp of straw on it. If there were any chickens you felt they'd be made to tiptoe round the edges. Every window gleamed and shone and the curtains hung down inside, stiff as paper. Paper flowers in brass pots stood on the sills. The square flag-stones up to the shiny, beetly, black front door looked as if they'd been scaled with hard wire wool.

Harry hung back from this house but his mother walked very carefully up these bleached stones. She knocked very quietly. After a minute she said, "I expect everyone has gone to the sea here too," and knocked rather loud, and at the very same second out of the kennel by the garden gate sprang a great black dog with yellow eyes and teeth and a long clanking chain. He pounced on Harry, and the great black door swung back in one sweep and out came a big square woman in a sombre dress. She had steely hair and eyes and mouth and wiry whiskers.

Harry's mother flew to Harry and the dog pounced towards both of them, straining the chain, prancing on mad feet and yelping with a mad mouth. The woman – after a time – told it to give over. She did not move her gaze from Harry or his mother for a moment and she did not move.

"Oh I'm so sorry – I'm so sorry. Were you – resting?"

"I was reading," said the woman.

"Oh – I'm sorry to disturb – "

"Reading my Bible."

"Oh dear. Oh – it was – well, it was eggs."

"Eggs?"

"I was told. Back in the village. You sell eggs."

"I do."

"And I've run out of eggs. And it's always scrambled eggs for supper on Sunday. Or tins. We're on holiday."

"Where from?" said the steel woman. In time. She arranged her hands criss-cross over her stomach.

"From London."

"I shouldn't care to live in London. Where are you stopping?"

"We're above the quarry. At old Mr Hewitson's farm, Light Trees. We lease it. They're all away today at the sea."

This seemed to make the woman very disgruntled. She turned away from them and said, breathing deeply, "How many eggs?"

"Oh – three dozen."

"Three *dozen!*"

"Yes. Well. There's a lot of us. We have a lot of friends coming and going."

"Have you a basket?"

Harry's mother had forgotten all about a basket. Mrs Teesdale always gave her egg boxes.

"I will *lend* you a basket," said the stern, broad woman. She turned her eyes on the dog which at last stopped sobbing and yelping and slunk back in to its kennel. Then she removed her crossed hands from her stomach, clenched her fists, turned her back on them and walked away.

"Why is it Blue Barns when all's black?" asked Harry.

"Hush."

"And why's she got metal whiskers?"

"Hush."

"I'm thirsty."

"Hush."

The woman came back with a big shallow plaited basket more like a tray with thirty six-eggs laid out over it which were going to have a sea-sick time up Quarry Hill.

"Can I have a drink of water?" asked Harry – who was

always good – in a bossy voice.

"Hush," said his mother again, "we'll go home for tea. Or –" she said, more daring since they were almost escaped now, "or could you tell us? Is there somewhere round about where we could get some tea?"

"*Get* some tea?"

"Well, where they serve teas. Teas. In the South you can see it advertised. TEAS."

The woman stood quite still.

"On notices," said Harry's mother getting feebler. "By road sides. TEAS. With cakes and things," and her voice trailed away.

"*I* can give you some tea," said the woman. "Step this way."

Harry – who was always good – retreated very fast down the path and hid behind the garden gate. His mother had to run and grab him. "Step this way," said the woman again and dismally they had to follow through the black door in to the very clean house to the very clean parlour and sit at a very polishy table among the brass pots and vases and everlasting flowers, upright chairs and any number of photographs of people in wedding dresses and all with the bristle-woman's jaw. A clock ticked like tin cans and hanging above it was a great piece of writing made of woollen stitches and decorated all round with dark brown woollen flowers. The writing said YE KNOW NOT THE HOUR.

In the silence that fell in the boiling airless room you could hear bread being cut far off in the kitchen and the slow clatter of a kettle. Harry put his head on the table and fell asleep.

The tea when it came was very ample.

But rather dry.

Plate after plate the steely woman brought – once or twice

she brought three plates at once, one on top of the other joined together with wires. Different kinds of pale heavy cake lay on these. All the things looked rather old though they were definitely home-made. They had been built, like the bristle woman herself, to last.

The butter was marg.

A giant pot of tea arrived.

Harry asked again for a glass of water. Or orange.

"Milk," said the bristle woman and brought milk and went away again.

Harry – who was always good – said in a minute, "I can't drink it."

"Oh Harry!"

"It tastes of meat."

"Don't be silly. Let me try."

It tasted of meat.

"She's had it in a fridge near meat. Crowding it up. She's mean. I want water. And it's horrible marg on the bread."

"Oh Harry."

"I can't eat the bread. The marg tastes of meat, too."

"Shall I ask for some jam?"

Harry's mother went to the door and coughed. Immediately in the opposite door across the passage stood the woman.

"Oh – do you think we might have a little – jam?"

"*Jam?*" said the woman. "Well – jam. I'll have to go to my store cupboard."

"Oh please –" But too late.

In time she arrived with delicious home-made black currant. "*That's* better," said appalling Harry – who was always good – and dug deep down in it and got a fair dollop on the table cloth and several smears about the hair and mouth. He met the bristle lady's glare with his clear eyes. In time once more, she went away.

"We'd better go," said Mrs Bateman looking through the

tight shut window at the stand-still day. "Long walk home. And with eggs it will be slow."

The woman appeared with the tray of eggs and handed it to Harry. "Oh thank you so very much and the jam was *lovely*," said his mother very courteously. "How much do we owe you."

"Oh I can't take pay on a Sunday," said the woman. "You must come and bring the money tomorrow. We're Chapel people here. I can only *give* you the eggs today. You must pay tomorrow."

"Oh, I'm so sorry, I didn't know. I didn't understand. Of course we'll come tomorrow when we return the tray. I'll send some of the big boys on their bikes. You should —"

"It is a sin to buy and sell on a Sunday."

"Yes. I see. Of course. And do tell me how much we should bring. And how much we owe you for the tea."

"For the *tea*?" The woman's eyes pierced in to Harry's mother's muddly kind face. "For the *tea*? I don't take any money for teas. I'm a long way from needing to serve *teas*. The tea was a kindness."

Harry's mother's mouth fell open in shame (Oh the jam! She had *asked* for the jam. And it had been an *invited* tea!).

Harry stretched up a hand to hold hers as they stood once more outside the front door.

"By the by," said the woman, "didn't I see the lad had left his milk? Would you not like him to come back and finish the milk? Waste is a sin."

So Harry — who was always good — let go of his mother's hand and put his own on the tray of eggs. Then he took his other hand off the handle of the tray of eggs. Then he turned the tray of eggs over and watched them drop to the ground. Thirty-six big fresh farm eggs. They splatted with thirty-six splats on to the white scrubbed stones. Every one of them broke and ran except for perhaps three or four and these Harry chased as they rolled and he jumped on them.

Then he jumped and he stamped with his feet on all the eggs until his sandals were slidy and slimy and juicy yellow and left great sticky messes down the path.

Far and away he ran, down the path, past the dog, out of the gate, down the lane. Down the lane to the three lane ends and his mother after him. "Harry!" she cried down the dark narrow, flowery lane. No sign of him.

Faster and faster she ran crying "Harry" at every bend; but every bend showed only the white ruts and the clutched fingers of the rose branches overhead and the red spikes of the nightshade laughing at her from the deep grass banks. She shot out of the lane on to Gypsies' Hill. But the gypsies were gone.

Their fire smoked white ash. There was a good deal of rubbish left. But the vans and cans and the pony and the line of washing might never have been. GYPSIES PROHIBITED spoke out from the post, and the gypsies were gone.

And so was Harry.

"Harry! Harry!" his mother shouted. He couldn't have got this far so fast. She ran and ran – still no Harry. Past the pub and the cluster of houses and into Jingling Lane and still no Harry. Oh, she thought – Harry gagged and bound. Away with the gypsies. He loves gypsies. "Hello my lovely," they'd said, and he'd waved and said "Hello."

"HARRY," she shrieked and ran down Jingling Lane and into the village lane and into the village, sure now that Harry's short legs could not have got this far alone. "KIDNAPPED," she shrieked at Jimmie Meccer, who blinked and pointed.

For there he was – and so were the Teesdales and old Grandad Hewitson laughing, and Jimmie Meccer laughing, tottering and peeping from his shed, and the four proud upset hens putting their necks out of the hedge again and village people waking up as it grew cooler and looking out round curtains to see what the noise was about, and the

31

blood red lupins standing watching and Mrs Teesdale in her sugar pink holiday hat.

As Mrs Bateman puffed up, the car with the rest of the Batemans came over the bridge too and Harry rather tended to wander out of sight again when he saw his father coming.

But somehow all was laughter.

"You never – you never went asking favours at Blue Barns," said Mr Teesdale. "Dearie me – it's prayers only there on a Sunday. None the worse I dare say, but it's not a place for jollifications."

"She was *awful*. She said she'd give us tea and then she wouldn't let us pay. And she said she'd give us eggs but it was a sin if we paid before tomorrow. She just let us make mistakes. She *watched* us making mistakes. She enjoyed us making mistakes. Harry was dreadful. She brought out dreadful things in him. You'd not believe – I just don't understand people up here."

"You understand us," said Mrs Teesdale, "and you're coming in for a proper tea and some eggs in boxes." Which they did, and the milk didn't taste of meat and the butter wasn't marg and there was the most tremendous lot to talk about.

"Should we ask Jimmie Meccer in?" said Mr Teesdale.

"That we will not," said his wife. "Letting them go asking favours of that witch."

"You'd best take a scrubbing brush with you," said Mrs Teesdale as they left, "unless you've got one up there at Light Trees. Harry'll need it tomorrow when he goes back to scrub her path – though she'll have done it by then herself of course."

"She will," said Grandad Hewitson. "First stroke after Sunday midnight she'll be out on her knees on them stones."

"How much for the eggs?" asked Mrs Bateman.

"Tell you later," said Mrs Teesdale.

Back at Light Trees, late in the long light evening, Harry

was singing happily on the horse rake and his parents were hanging over the sheep pens, watching the sun go down behind the Castle Farm below, where the Lord of the Marches must have seen it sometimes too, looking much as it did tonight, and said as they did, "What a day it has been – and I'd think it would be hot again tomorrow." Perhaps the mother and child curled up under the bridge had sometimes said the same.

"We saw the gypsies again today," said Harry's mother. "First they were there, then they were gone. Like magic. I think they put a spell on Harry. I've never known him so naughty. Or maybe it was that woman. Did you hear Mrs Teesdale say she was a witch?"

"Rubbish."

"She was funny about selling eggs. Very superstitious, that. Perhaps she is a witch after all."

"No different from Mrs Teesdale. Didn't you notice? She wouldn't take money from you today either."

"She was different from Mrs Teesdale. Mrs Teesdale spares your blushes. And she makes you laugh. In her pink hat."

"The pink hat makes the difference? If the egg-witch woman had a pink hat – ?"

"Let's buy her one."

"She'd paint it black."

Harry behind them was content upon the horse rake. He swung it up high in the sky over the fells and looked down on the sleeping land. He droned happily to himself as he wheeled and swung high in the sky with the pale stars beginning to show. He wondered why they had had to go out visiting for tea when there was a horse rake and Light Trees to play in.

3 · Sweep

The chimney sweep, who also kept the fish and chip shop, had said that he would take the big London lads fishing one day and they had said thank you. Smashing. "Oh great," they had said – and forgotten. They weren't prepared then on a dark wet August day for a knock on Light Trees' ancient oak door and the sweep – Kendal was his name – to be standing there sopped through, with floods streaming from his hat and his arms full of rods.

It was a day when great curtains of rain swept the fells and away and away stretched dismal wet hills. Everyone of the London folk, even the mother, was still in bed with books and breakfast and the radio at nine o'clock. The little lad, Harry, was in bed with a lego set and a gang of invisible friends. It was Harry who heard the sweep knock, the front door being under one of his bedroom windows.

"Fishing," Kendal called up to him, wet as a man under the sea.

"Any chips?" asked Harry.

"Haven't caught any yet. Chips is hard to catch. And the opposite sort of an affair."

"Opposite?"

"Aye – you throw chips in the deep end. Fish you fishes out. Can I step inside? I'm taking the big lads fishing."

Various older boys of terrible appearance emerged from the bedroom where they had all been put in together to keep the mess in one place. One was eating bread and marmalade, one was holding a paper-back western. James, the tall thin Bateman one, was doing nothing but look vacant. Tremendous pop music flooded out from behind them and out of the front door across the mournful landscape.

"Isn't it too wet?" James said doubtfully.

"Wet is what's needed for trout," said the sweep.

"They'll catch pneumonia," said Mrs Bateman fussing round in a clutched-up dressing gown to get the sweep a cup of coffee.

"Not at all," he said. "Never int' world. I never yet met a trout with pneumonia. These lads tell me they like the thought of fishing every time they come in my shop. It happens that there's this day free, people not being over-fond of having their chimneys swept with dampness about."

The dampness flung itself against the kitchen windows like tidal waves. A tempest of wind shrieked.

"I think I ought to do some work," said James. "It's a chance, a day like this. I've got exams you see." He slunk back in to the bedroom and his friends kept well out of the foreground too.

"I'll come," said Harry.

"No you will not," said his mother, "you can't swim."

"Oh, it'll not come to that," said Kendal. "We just wade. Only deep places is whirlpools and once in whirlpools swimming's of little advantage."

The mother waved a coffee pot helplessly about, looking urgently at her husband who had just appeared in pyjamas, unshaven with his hair very early-morning. "Aha," he said. "Ha. Early call? Yes. Good to see you, Kendal. Forgotten I'd mentioned the chimney. Rather wet for it today, I'd think."

"It's fishing," said the mother. "Kendal wants to take everyone fishing. Just the weather, he says."

"Wonderful idea," said the father. "Great. Grand. Couldn't think what on earth to do with any of them today. Splendid. We can knock up a few sandwiches for everyone, can't we? It'll be an all day affair?" he asked hopefully.

"It will," said Kendal, "and you're welcome to come with us."

"Ah well now then," said the father, "it just happens that I can't. There's a phone call coming from abroad. I have to wait for it." He looked out at the deluge. "Great pity," he said. "Long time since I had a day's fishing."

"The telephone lines are down," said Kendal. "The wind took them in the night. You'd mebbe hear it happening? Two trees across the Appleby road an' all and a cargo of dead sheep strowed about all over it. Like an air disaster. Vet had to go and put them out of their misery. There'll be no phone calls."

Mr Bateman gave Kendal a look, picked up the phone, found it dead and gave him another look. "Yes," he said. He glared thoughtfully at Kendal as if Kendal had arranged the wind and Kendal stared serenely back. He was a short, broad man with a wide mouth and dauntless shoulders. He strikingly resembled the stone figure that had been dug up in the church-yard some years ago – a very early Saxon hackabout of the devil in chains. Bound hand and foot, this stone demon looks entirely comfortable, watching the torturer with an expression of the purest happiness. Queer words carved beneath mean 'Beware or cop it'.

It was possible that the model for this stone had been an earlier member of the Kendal family for it had been discovered in a field below the church and Kendals had always lived below the church. "Well, since thirteenth century anyway," he said. "A very funny class of persons lives above." And if you weren't careful he began to tell stories about them. All Kendals told superb stories, this Kendal in particular, and while he told them you found that you were going along with him in a sort of dream and had bought five pounds worth of fish and chips or seven fishing rods displayed in his window beside the bottles of vinegar and tomato ketchup; or had contracted to have your chimneys swept twice yearly till the turn of the century.

Or as now – he had started on an account of last night's storm: a tree struck by lightning in Jingling Lane that he'd heard tell had flattened the vicar; Blue Barns' roof blown in whilst madam was out on her broomstick. And you found yourself trudging off towards his land rover and the river to catch trout, wet, cold, ill-tempered as any group of prisoners in the world, when all you wanted was bed and toast and Radio Two. Harry and his mother who had been expected to stay behind were left with a built-up fire at Light Trees and a comfortable quiet morning.

And afternoon, so it appeared, for there was no sign of the fishermen by four o'clock.

And evening – for there was no sign of them by seven.

Mrs Bateman had done Normandie potatoes and the lovely smell of cheese and onions floated out of the windows and up the chimney and under the front door and away over the fell. "You'd think it'd tempt them home," she said. But the river was far below and four miles westwards. "Hot air only rises," said Harry. "Only the birds'll know it's Normandie potatoes and they're not bothered."

"Don't say 'Not bothered'," said his mother. "Don't talk like Bell, nice as he is. And there's not a bird flying any more than there has been all day. It's a day for neither human, animal, bird or fish. Ridiculous the whole thing."

"Completely ridiculous," she said rather later. "Your father was feeble not standing up to that sweep. He'll get a chest again. And James with his exam."

At seven she said, "Ridiculous, reckless, unwise and *jeopardising* his work" – for the telephone had revived and New York had just rung at the time it had arranged for a vital discussion. There had been great difficulty in getting through, said New York.

"The lines have been down," said Harry's mother. "We are having very bad weather here."

"Then why is he out in it?" New York asked and rang off.

"Call this a holiday," Mrs Bateman cried as she often did.

At half past nine there was a scuffly sound over the yard and the scrape of a catch of a gate. Then subdued and squelching feet slowly plodded over stone flags. Hungry Harry and his mother beheld the group standing with pools spreading about their feet, long faces drooping below drooping hats, rods held dipped like flags at a funeral. From Mr Bateman's left hand hung four trout, so small and of such depressed appearance that they could have hardly tugged. Fish, one felt, that had been hanging about waiting for death.

"It is nearly ten o'clock at night," screamed Harry's mother.

She seized the fishes, flew to the kitchen, whacked off their heads, whipped out their insides, swished them with butter and flung them under the grill.

"Four between six. Four between seven if Kendal's staying. Where is Kendal?"

"Here I am," he stepped cheerfully in, "rather late. Never mind. Four fine trout. They weren't rising today in any numbers."

"I've been frantic – frantic, Kendal. All alone with the baby – Harry – up here in the mist."

"Even so – even so – a grand day."

"Frantic. Lonely. And the phone rang! There you are now. The phone rang. They're furious with you. What a holiday. You'll have lost it. Lost the job."

"A fair day tomorrow I'd think," said Kendal, shutting the door on the outside world, "fairing up every minute. We must keep – "

She disappeared in to the kitchen to turn the trout. The rest of the party staggered upstairs towards hot water. Kendal stood by himself in the porch dripping and smiling at Harry.

" – keep our heads," he finished. "Unlike the poor trout. Not wise to remove their heads," he said to Harry. "The finest taste is in the cheeks."

"Teaching me to cook fish now," Mrs Bateman fumed to herself in the kitchen, "I'm being treated like a fool." The four fish looked smaller every minute. "Will you stay for supper, Kendal?" she called bleakly.

"That'd be grand," he said. "Just the thing."

"Though I dare say Mrs Kendal may be worrying?" She put her hot face round the kitchen door. "I expect you feel you ought to go home to Mrs Kendal?"

"Oh not at all. Not at all. She knows my ways."

Salad, bread, butter, cheese appeared on the table with Harry's sleepy help, mayonnaise, wine, water and the four fish, now looking like minnows. The big dish of Normandie potatoes put in the middle. They had got very crusty.

"Serve them right and serve them right," said Mrs Bateman crossly. Feeling like the Egg Witch she crossed her hands on her apron and said, "That's all there is."

"Mrs Kendal sent up something," said Kendal as the rest of the family shambled in with the bright pink slippery exhausted look that comes at the end of a day's wind and rain and open air and ineffectiveness. Mr Bateman considered how stupid he was, not even being able to stay in and wait for a phone call. James considered what it was going to feel like when he'd failed his exam. The other boys considered how unwise they had been to come up here to this wet bit of England for their holidays. Their hostess considered how unmarried women with wonderful jobs have a better time of it, and who, if they knew, would be silly enough to have children. Harry considered how much he loved Mr Kendal the sweep who never got out of sorts and here he was coming from his land rover carrying a covered basket.

"Salmon," he said. "Brought it up this morning in the car from the wife. Cold enough in there to stay fresh in this weather, and cooked all ready to eat, with peppercorns and bay leaves."

A glorious cold salmon slid out of the basket on a long dish and was placed upon the table. "Wow!" said several people at once, and "Oh my goodness!" said Mrs Bateman blushing pink.

"But food is not enough," said Mr Kendal, "to save a day. Especially a day like this one. Just hark!"

Rain still beat on the little house on the fell and the wind knocked and pushed ominously at the chimney pot. "Sometimes," said Kendal, "I'd reckon it was worse up here in August than at any other time. There's something demented about dark storms in mid-summer. More salmon – yes indeed. All must be consumed. Food does go some distance towards happiness in bad weather. My, but I've not ever eaten such grand potatoes."

"Oh, I'll miss the potatoes for the salmon any time," said the London father. "We can eat potatoes at home."

"Then I'll have the recipe for Mrs K.," said the sweep. "We grow tired of chips."

One of James's London friends said he couldn't believe in being tired of chips, though the salmon was wonderful.

"So's the little fishes," said Harry.

"But not enough. Not enough," said Kendal, "like I and the Bible were saying. Not even on a dark night with good friends in an old house with the wind round it. Food is not enough. There's things I could tell you about this house, given time."

"Is it haunted?" said James.

"Not at all. Not like yonder. But there's a tale or two – "

"Where is yonder?" Mr Bateman leaned back in his chair and sighed with pleasure for he felt so fit and well – the fresh rain, the clean air, the salmon, the family all around him ("Yes – up in the north again this year. Oh yes – terrible weather but good for fishing. For trout fishing you know rain is what we like," he was saying in his mind, back in London).

"Where is yonder?"

"Oh – here and there. Just about everywhere round here. Plentiful ghost stories in Stainmer and North Westmorland. Deficient in much but plentiful in stories. Some of them old 'uns. None I'd say not known to me. Kendals has been here six hundred years and they say we've never done much or made money, but the one thing we do aright is tell stories. Apart from fish, that is, and sweep. They're all fairly ancient occupations."

"Were there chimneys in the thirteenth century?"

"There were Kendals so there were chimneys," said Kendal. "Well, Kendals probably got called in long before – to the Celts, messing about with holes in the roof and doors fore and aft for winnowing grain. Very dangerous and unscientific but you can't expect a great deal of Celts. Some of them peat hags is as old as Celts. You can probably pick out their spade marks. There's a Celtic settlement above this house."

"*Now?*" suddenly said Harry.

"Oh yes. Still there. Just a ring of green old turf now. Kind of place you could position machine guns if you've a mind."

"Would they have had fires? Celts up there?"

"They'd have died of cold else," said Kendal. "Curious old wig-wam things they had – like wild Indians. You can see them still if you look over Yorkshire way on the moors. Mind you, them fellers were real savages, them Celts. No better than Russians. Maybe they were Russians."

"Maybe Kendals were Russians," said one of James's friends.

Kendal looked very put out.

"You mean you wouldn't have cleaned their chimneys if they were Celts?" said Mr Bateman thinking out a short article for his paper.

"We would but we'd have charged the more."

"You mean then that if a Welsh family or an Irish family came to a holiday cottage up here you'd charge more than you do us? From London where we can be anything? That's most interesting. And I'm afraid it's racism."

"No it ain't," said Kendal, "no Welsh family would come up here to start with and the only Irishman I ever saw on North or South Stainmer or Hartley or Nateby Birket had to leave after a week on account of the farm having good bath, sink and taps but he'd omitted to see if there was water."

"It was not kind of you not to tell him," said the London mother. "Would you have told a Welshman?"

"A Welshman would have been too proud to ask. And if it was a Scotsman – though it wouldn't have been – we'd have said the house was sold already."

"That *is* racism," said Mrs Bateman. "It's dreadful. It's what people say about the north of England. The trouble is you can never tell if you're joking. I must say you've always been very kind to us." (She thought briefly of a first fuming hay-time when abominable things had nearly happened.)

"There's reasons for that," said Kendal.

"What?" James asked – because it's always nice to know why people like you.

"One," said Kendal, "you eat local. You don't come stacked up with London frozen stuff. Two, because you're not too grand to pass the time of day, and three" – he thought of the London mother's very nice letter of apology two or three years back which every one had heard about above and below the church and as far away as Mallerstang and Whaw – "because you're sociable folk. Which is more than can be said for some visitors and incomers. Did you ever hear of the incomer over Stainmer Old Spital?"

"Never," said all of them – all but Harry, full of fish on the sofa, who had fallen asleep like a kitten.

"Wait a moment," said his mother, "I'll make some tea. Clear the worst away all of you and we'll wash up tomorrow. Some of you stack up the fire. Mr Kendal do please take off those wellington boots – you're sure you won't ring Mrs Kendal? It's eleven o'clock at night."

"She knows me thank you. I'll be moving the minute I've finished my tale. But not till – for it's a tale you should hear from me or you'll go reading it in some book or other published in Oxford and Cambridge or Cardiff and places and no good for owt but reference libraries.

"Now then –

Sweep

"On a night not unlike this one a couple of hundred years ago there was a knock on a door not unlike the one behind me as I'm sitting. A door at the top of some stone stairs, a flight not unlike that of Light Trees again. The old farmer answered the door and let in an old woman in a long black cloak. She blew in rather than walked in, groaning and complaining. Groaning and complaining about being lost on Stainmer, that was no more of a friendly place then than it is now, and it was a night not fit for Christians. Not fit for devils.

"The old farmer's wife gave the poor thing a bowl of milk and showed her the kitchen settle to sleep on – they were very used to lost travellers – and they all went to bed.

"And the wind howled and the rain lashed – rather after the style of now – and no fish mind, no wine, no grand french potatoes. No electrics in the kitchen – only tallow candles and the dogs howling as guardians in the yard. Very noisy restive dogs they were too that night. The farmer twice thought he'd get out there to them to quiet them but it were late and he were tired and so he slept.

"Now there were a servant girl – and my granny knew her. When that lass were an old woman my granny knew her, so what about that? She had no room to herself them days but slept int' kitchen by the fire back, twirled up in a bit of a blanket. Lil'e wee bit of a lass, so small it's likely the old traveller din't see her at the start. Sharp-eyed lass, however, for lying there int' fire back she sees, on a level with her eyes, that this old woman, all bent over double, had the biggest female feet you ever did see – and she were wearing man's boots!

"'Hello,' says the little lass to herself – and she watches. Next she listens. Out of the pocket of her cloak the old woman takes a candle. All's quiet – even the dogs without. So she stands up straight and she flings off the cloak, and underneath there's the figure of a great, strong, ferocious

43

ruffian of a man.

"The man then takes from his pockets something small and solid and unwraps it from a rag, and the girl sees – that it's a human hand. Pale grey. A greasy thing not unlike the candle. The man places the candle in the fingers of the dead hand, and he lights it. The candle stays fixed in the fingers. Then this hand the ruffian sticks in a jar. He slowly bends over the girl he's just that moment seen and he passes the light before her eyes. Then he says these words,

> 'Let those who rest more deeply sleep:
> Let those awake their vigil keep.
> Oh Hand of Glory, shed thy light,
> Direct us to our spoil tonight' –

and there's not a child at Stainmer or in Kirkby school nor yet a conductress on the G.N.E. buses over Stainmer doesn't know that verse to this day. So what happens?"

The London mother was sitting up straight.

"He walks to the window, draws back the curtain and holding the candle he says,

> 'Flash out thy light, oh skeleton hand,
> And guide the feet of our trusty band'

and the light shoots up as if there's been pure cane sugar put on it, and the man walks to the door, draws back the bolts and steps outside to call in his assistant thieves. And he whistles.

"And up jumps the little lass, runs to the door and pushes him wham-bang in the middle of his back off the top of the steps and thump in to the yard. Then she runs in and bolts the door and tries to wake the family up.

"But the spell is still on them – the candle still burning. So she picks up the bowl of milk and pours it over the candle and out it goes – it wouldn't go out with blowing – and ten shakes of a whisker and the family's up and down stairs and firing off blunderbusses from the window. There's groans and terrible cries from down below in the yard and some sort

44

of a talk going on, and at last one of them, the leader of the gang, shouts up, 'Give up the Hand of Glory and we shall not harm you.' Off go the blunderbusses again however from the farm windows and a number of strong remarks, I'd reckon, and the thieves ran off.

"Now that hand and that candle were in the inn called The Old Spital over Stainmer many a long year. The hand is in the Whitby Museum to this day. And I hear tell there's another one in a museum westward."

Mr Kendal picked up his tea cup and finished his tea, looking very satisfied and lively.

"I am glad," said the London father, Mr Bateman, "that Harry is asleep."

"I don't like it," said one of James's London friends, "I don't much like that story. I don't know that I believe it either."

"It's an old one. It's a story you can hear with little differences all along the old Bowes Road. The candle had to be made from the fat of a hanged man. The flame held in the hand was unquenchable."

"It reminds me of something," said Mr Bateman, "it reminds me of another story – a light in a dead hand. Why but it's Roman, Kendal, isn't it? Or it might even be Ancient Greek."

"It's both," said Kendal. "Both. The Romans had it from the Greeks and when the Romans came a-conquering up here and sat for years in all the signalling posts along the road between Penrith and Greta Bridge they told it to all of us – giving thanks no doubt that they were among civilised folk and not on that other road farther north built by Hadrian where there was hardly a human being fit to tell a tale to. They told the story hereabouts again and again over the years, long after the Romans left. And there was still a trade in dead hands a hundred year ago. Well, my granny knew that servant. Bella, her name was. Old George Alderson was her master. Not very long since – just between the wars – there was a hand discovered in somebody's thatch over in Yorkshire. They were taking down the thatch to put a tile roof on after he'd died, and they found the hand hidden. He'd been a very rich feller, the owner of the house. Nobody had known where he got his money from, nor why he were always out at night."

"That story, Kendal," said the London father, ruminating, "must be old as Agamemnon. It's a wonderful story."

"Aye," said Kendal, "folks do get excited by it. I thought it might amuse."

"I don't know about amuse exactly," said the London mother, picking up Harry and carrying him off to bed, and shivering.

"Well, no," said Kendal, "it's a bit of a chestnut to tell you the truth round here. There's one or two more I could tell you more guaranteed for shuddering. Ghosts and horrors. As for things that has happened here in your house of Light Trees – my, but if you knew about the dead body that once lay in your dairy yonder for two weeks in the snow, stiff as a board on your cheese shelf – "

"I'll say goodnight, Mr Kendal."

"Stiff as a tree among the hams and the Wensleydale. Poor old chap, he'd be Joss Atkinson's auntie's father, they couldn't get him down to the cemetery. They sledged him down at last, right down Quarry Hill to the carpenter's. Made a sledge from old bits of your cow stalls in the byre – you can still see the marks out there if you look. Dreadful thing to do you know. That cow house is eighteenth century woodwork – the stable's got carved columns would grace a church. Oh this is a very historical house you've found. There's folks watching you through every chink."

"*Goodnight*, Mr Kendal."

"And I daresay you're going to greatly enjoy it over the years and time to come yourselves'll be looking out of the chinks at others now unborn."

"*Goodnight.* Mind the steps. Watch your feet over the yard. Can we light you to the gate?"

The wind and rain had stopped at last. It was a still, black night. Not a light to be seen, not a star in the sky. The roadless fells rolled like unseen seas all about them as they stood on the old stone outdoor staircase. From far below and far away came up the twelve strokes of the Kirkby church bell as it had struck for hundreds of years.

"Midnight," said Kendal. "End of a grand and cheerful day."

4 · The Hollow Land

Bell and Harry lay on their stomachs in the Celtic Camp, like machine-gunners, looking over the landscape at James far below them.

James sat on another slope beneath a crag with a book open on his knees and in turn watched a figure below him – old Grandfather Hewitson who was parading along the dry bed of a beck, slashing thistles.

The four figures were the only signs of life for miles. It was a hot, still day. Light Trees was the only building in sight. No smoke rose from its chimney. Far away the Lake District mountains swam with heat.

"However long is it going to be?" said Harry. "He could sit there all day. And when he does get hungry and go in, there's still your grandad."

"You'd think he'd know every word of that book by now," said Bell. "Does he do owt else but take exams?"

"Not much," said Harry, "he's good at them."

"Not surprised, the time he spends."

"He's talking to your grandad now. Look, he's put the book down. Maybe he'll forget it and they'll go off together somewhere. Maybe he'll start helping your grandad thistle."

"I doubt. Grandad's talking back at him now. He's leaning on the scythe. James is in for a session. We'll not get there today. We'd best give up and do summat different."

"Oh no. No! Let's wait on. He can't sit there forever. We mightn't ever get another chance. All of them off to Penrith or London or walking, and nobody coming after us."

"Are you sitting there forever, Slim Jim?" said Old Hewitson to James on the lower level.

"Till I know this chapter," said James.

"Chapter eh?"

"Exams. It's work. I've got to work this holiday."

"Work eh?"

"Science."

"Science eh? I never seemed to hear much in my day about Science. It must be enjoyable. 'Thou doesn't look as though thou's working when thou *is* working' as my father used to say to the travelling tinker." He leaned on the short handle that stuck out of the long handle of the huge scythe and took a coloured handkerchief out of his pocket and tied it round his head. His large red face grinned piratically beneath. One of his blue eyes looked at the wide and silent fell and the other down at the thistles. The fells were pink with drought and the only sparkle came from the white of the salt-lick blocks for the thirsty cattle under the grey and silver trunks of the may trees. "Unusual hot," he said, looking intently at the bumpy outline of the Celtic Camp. "Unusual quiet. Must be grand for you after London. Not that I've ever been there. Grand having nothing to do."

"My mother says there's plenty to do. Same old shopping and cooking and washing – and the washing's more trouble because you have to take it four miles to the launderette. And my father has plenty to do. He writes for newspapers. He's had to go to London today."

Old Hewitson considered this. Then he gave a sweep of the scythe and eight huge thistles toppled like towers. He was a short-legged, large-headed man like a gnome and not only did his eyes look in different directions, his feet had something of the same complaint. One of them seemed to press down deeper than the other. Like Rumpelstiltskin he had the look of somebody who had just stamped. The scythe, which he swung again, and again down crashed a city, was much taller than he was. He walked away up the beck swinging it and turned and came swinging back again.

"Unusual, unusual, unusual hot," he said. "Day for the sea-side. Not that I were ever there above twice and the last time two year ago when that Harry had the fight with the Egg Witch and there was better entertainment at home. I'd not weep and die if I never saw the sea more."

He took a water-bottle out of somewhere inside his trousers and offered James a drink.

"It's all right. I'm going in to get some lunch soon." He looked at the thistles – fat and lush, silver-grey and copper-lavender in the sun. "Funny," he said, "so many thistles."

"Funny's what it's not."

"They ought to have discovered a selective weed killer."

"They have, it's called a donkey."

"Why doesn't Mr Teesdale get a donkey?"

"He's got one. It's called Old Hewitson."

"What's thou laughing at?" he added. "Come on now. Stir thy sinews. Take a swipe and leave that exam. What is it anyway?"

"Geology. The study of rocks."

"Rocks eh?" He gave another two-way glare at the Celtic Camp. "Come on. Take a swipe."

James put down the book, slid off the bank and took a

great swing with the scythe.

"LOOK OUT," cried Old Hewitson leaping the beck, "are you right?"

"Nothing much," said James rolling about in agony and holding his shin.

"Take my head-band. Bind it tight. It's not over damp. You'll be right in a half hour. It's not work for a tawny-ket. Nor yet was Tommy Littlefair's but that was because it was too far the other way for the leg was a gonner. Survived splendid mind. The only wooden-legged man I ever knew to ride a bicycle. What's that you said about thistles being funny?"

James lay and rolled on the beck bank looking pale, and far above Harry said, "Your grandad's cut James's leg off. Shall we go down?"

"We'll move in closer," said Bell, "while they're off guard. Come on. Sideways and down in to the ravine and over the broken fence. Then up and round behind them. If he can still walk they'll maybe go now."

"You'd think your grandad would want his lunch. He's been out since about dawn."

"He eats on the hoof. Why he has to thistle there today I don't know. And why your brother has to choose that very bouse to sit on and do his exams I don't know."

"Is the opening right near then?"

"Right near."

"And they've never seen it? Not even your grandfather, living here all his life?"

"It wasn't there all his life. It's a shift in the earth. He's not been able to get up the bouse since the day he got his leg flattened. Not even my dad knows about the opening and there's not much he doesn't know. He knows about the pit-head mind. Well even you've seen that. The pit-head's obvious, once you've walked in the cave in the fell side. You

51

can't miss that opening with them great iron bars over it. But not even my dad knows about the overhead hole up beyond. You can't get a tractor up there and I've seen to it no sheep gets stuck in it. I put a slab over."

"Have you ever been down?"

"Aye. Once. With a rope. We shan't need a rope today being two of us. I never been along inside though. It's no place to be in alone. Mind we're not going far inside today neither. We just walk around a bit and climb out again."

"But you said there's a railway in there. A real one."

"Aye."

"With lines."

"Rails. And little trucks."

"Little trucks? Go on. Tell on."

"What?"

"What you tell't before."

"Told before. All I said was there was silver there. It's a silver mine. You can see the silver glints in the walls. Down further there'll be long layers of it. They never finished working it out. There's poison down there. In the channels of the rails. All running."

"Could we get it out? The silver?"

"Don't be daft. You had to have worked twenty years before you were trusted to knock out the real stuff."

They had left the Celtic Camp far behind them now and dropped off the fell in to a deep cleft. James and Old Hewitson were out of sight. They began to climb the far side of the cleft pulling themselves up by bushes and rocks. A sheep racketed away from them once from behind some gorse bushes and once a family of grouse shot up from under their feet making a noise like wooden rattles. Bell and Harry stood still for a minute, then fell on their stomachs and crawled to the edge of the crag top and looked down. James and Old Hewitson were much nearer now, directly below, but still too far off for Bell and Harry to catch their voices.

"See where your brother's left his book? He was sat not twenty feet below the hole if he did but know it. He might have been safer there than in the beck scything. Looks as if he's landed now for another hour. And so are we. Look."

Old Hewitson was bringing a picnic out of another compartment of his trousers and passing things to James.

"Are you right?"

"I'm all right," said James doubtfully, trying to stand.

"That's the lad. When Henry Cleesby got lamed on these fells he never sat up again. He got rolled on by his tractor liming the Quarry Field. And as for Jimmie Meccer, he's reduced to yon shed all day. Doesn't even let the doctor see his legs. Nothing of course to the old mining accidents. There's been mines up here since the Middle and Dark Ages you know. Accidents and various mysteries happened not a hundred yards from this spot even in my life-time. Now – what's this you say about thistles being funny?"

"Just –" said James, "just it's funny they're so big and juicy-looking when the ground's as dry as rock."

"The drier on top," said the old man, "the wetter below. The drier a place looks on these fells the deeper the water running secret beneath. This is hollow land."

"Hollow?"

"Listen."

They sat together in the burning, still morning, but James could hear nothing.

"I can hear nothing."

"Ah well."

"What is there to hear?"

"The rivers running. Way, way below the ground. But you're not practised. You'll not hear them yet. That's why you should never go pot-holing round here. Not unless you're with experts and know the tunnels like bees know the honeycombs. It's not only natural tunnels and channels under the fells, see. It's old mines. No one in their senses goes near them – nor anything else humans copies from nature, aeroplanes being no exception. There's no such thing as accidents – just clumsiness and daftness and butting in where nature knows best."

"This cut on my leg's an accident, isn't it?"

"No – clumsiness and daftness. Thy clumsiness and my daftness in letting you try a sickle without showing you how. No – there's no-one with one iota of sense that'd go down the old mines now. Roofs all caved in. Gases. Falling rock. Fumes. There's miles you could wander seeking a way out if you got lost and never be heard of more. The mine you've been sitting below has been sealed off solid these sixty years."

"Sitting below?"

"Aye. You were on the bouse – the tip at the mine mouth. Can't you see the slope's a different shape? Yon hump? Even different plants grow on it. Different lichens on the stones."

They both looked up at the bouse and Bell and Harry bobbed down their heads from the top of the crag above it.

The day had grown immensely still, immensely hot. There was a curious silence, the sky so blue that it seemed here and there to hold darkness in it, to be almost black.

"It's said to be haunted up here you know," said Old Hewitson. "Not many would come up here behind Light Trees at night. Me, I find there's more ghosts about in the day. On hot quiet days like this one. There's those say if you listen you can hear the old hammers going, the picks of the miners long ago, and the trucks running over the wooden rails. Now and then you can just about catch old voices with old words in them. Then there's the woman that's often seen walking. She walks just up yonder."

He pointed. Bell and Harry's heads bobbed down again. James's spine prickled right up to the back of his neck and then round to his cheeks.

"A ghost?"

"Aye. Likely. She goes walking in a white apron over the bouse. She walks to the top and shades her eyes and looks in all directions. Then she's gone. Just disappears. In to the sunshine. Nothing left but the air and the fell and the birds. Like a creature walking through water she is – Mrs Meccer used to say."

"Have you seen her?"

"Maybe once. That sweep, Kendal, makes out he's always seeing her – quite a friend of his. Our Eileen seed her once, too – the day the tractor rolled on Henry Cleesby. I seed her when I was about Harry's age, the day I got my leg flattened in the shift. Mrs Meccer seed her twice, but that's not surprising since it's her own grandmother."

"What – the woman is? The ghost is?"

"Aye. She was Mrs Meccer's gran out looking for her son. That's to say Mrs Meccer's uncle. He came on up here when he was a lad of sixteen or so. There was this family row and he goes storming out, like lads do that age, left his dinner half-eaten, grinds back his chair from the table. 'If that's how it is, I'se leaving home.' You know the sort of thing."

"Yes."

"Well, he goes storming up the fell. They never seed him more."

"What – he *disappeared*?"

"Aye. Long since. She never got over it. Walked the fells looking for him for days and nights. Then she died. But she goes on looking for him. You see her before there's some disaster. Walking quiet. Shading her eyes. In a white apron."

"I think I'll go in now. Can you give me a hand up?"

"Have I sobered you, young James? Well, I'se sorry. Dear me."

"No. Well – no. It's just coming over rather thundery. I think I'll go back up to Light Trees. It *is* rather a depressing sort of story."

"Oh don't worry about it. I'd say the lad took off some-where and made his fortune. The old woman was a right misery by all accounts."

"But still – " James looked up at the wide watchfulness of the fell.

"Oh, come on lad. We'll both get off. Why don't you come off over Stainmer with me and that Kendal this after-noon? We're jaunting. There's no harm can come to you up here you know if you don't do owt daft and slip-shod."

As the two of them turned away (both limping), Bell and Harry slid forward. Bell eased a huge slab of limestone from a slight dip in the ground, laying bare a hole that might have been a narrow fox-hole lying beneath a shelf of earth and quartz. Then he slid inside it and dropped in to the dark, turning to catch Harry who slid in to the dark beside him.

"Are we down?"

"Aye – but wait till I get – "

"It's not deep."

"Not yet. Wait. Where's the torch?"

"It's a queer smell."

"It gets worse. Nearer the trucks. Like dead bodies..Mind we're not going far. We take a quick look at them trucks and we go straight back. To get back you get on to my shoulders and I jump you up again. Then you lean down in and pull me out after. See?"

"Look." He turned his torch up to the faint light from the blazing day outside, then along the tunnel they stood in. They had dropped through its roof. Stones and rubble lay underfoot. The tunnel went in two directions, each in to deep darkness. The torch,when Bell shone it at the roof, picked out small glitters and spangles like frosted cobwebs.

"Is it real silver?"

"I'd say so."

"Already? But we can't be that far down inside?"

"The mines over Alston you can see the silver from the very pit-head. Just by looking through the bars of the grille-thing at the entrance. We went at our school. For History."

"Can we get some? Why did they leave it?"

"Not worth picking out, this lot. The stuff worth having is deep down. Miles down. They used to take folks down there for jaunts in the old days. All dolled-up folks. Rich folks. Used to go down for kicks, wrapped in fancy dust-sheets to see the poor miners slaving away. Used to travel down in the little wagons. Sat on little benches, screaming and hugging each other like in a ghost train."

"Why can't we go down?"

"Don't be soft. It's not maintained now. It's probably all fell in further off. We'd get down there and there'd be a shift and we be gonners. I'se not daft."

"What's a shift?"

"It's what you get round here. Limestone. Ask yon James. It'll be in his book. It was a shift when my grandad flattened his leg. In Light Trees' Home Field. It just suddenly rippled about and threw him down. Like someone moving about under blankets – some giant – he said. Rocks all came tumbling. They call them earthquakes in Japan. Hey – look. Here we are."

Walking one behind the other, one hand to the tunnel wall and the torch jerking here and there, Bell's foot had come up against something that wasn't rock.

"Here's the rails. Feel."

"They're not wood. They clank."

"They didn't *stay* wood. That was in old ancient times. This mine was in business not that long since. It only stopped when Grandad was a lad. It got too expensive and there was a war and that. Look."

The torch shone on the back of a little wagon. It was attached to another, and another. A little string of them.

Propped against the side of one was a fine large pick and a spade.

"Just left here. Just *left*. Look here – "

There were cans and buckets and a couple of spidery, rusty lanterns and two or three tin mugs.

"My – they must have left in a hurry. Fancy leaving all this when they was all poor and going to be out of jobs. What was that?"

"What?"

"Noise like a sort of a shower."

"I didn't hear."

"A sort of rumble. Oh!"

From behind them down the tunnel there came a long swishing noise. A sort of sigh, then silence.

"It sounded like water or something," said Harry.

"No. It'll not be water. It's dry enough."

"I've heard your grandad say. 'The drier above – ' "

"Aye. I know, ' – the wetter beneath'. But that's the underground rivers. There's no rivers down here. It's a ship-shape mine. It's dry as dry. Look." He shone the torch along the slope of the floor which was dry, though in the two runnels the rails were set in was a thick gluey white liquid like condensed milk.

"I don't like look of yon," said Harry.

Before Bell could correct the yon, there came from down the tunnel a very long and hostile swish and hiss – a sound like a great serpent stirring towards them from the bottom of the mine. Then a thundering long rumble, and a puff of something. They clung to the wagon, and their eyes and noses stung and they began to cough. After what seemed a long time the air cleared, and there was complete silence.

"What was it Bell?"

"We'd best go see."

They walked the little way back again to the hole they had dropped through, feeling the wall as it curved round and slightly down, and came to where they had started out. A solid barrier of earth and rocks completely blocked the tunnel. The hole in the roof, its edges loosened first by them and by the dryness of the earth around, had crumbled and dribbled and showered into the darkness below. First the soil, then smaller stones and then the huge chunks and blocks of rock had settled in tons into the space prepared for them.

There was no sign in the tunnel where five minutes ago they had looked up at the sky that the sun and the grasses and the sheep and the flying grouse were still passing a summer's day hardly ten feet above their heads.

And there was not the least chance in the world of getting out.

Mrs Bateman, back from Penrith with her arms full of clean washing and a lot of parcels, walked into Light Trees' kitchen and called "Harry?"

She looked in the back dairy and saw that the sandwiches for Harry's lunch were still under the pyrex dish and the apples and chocolate lay uneaten beside them. He'll be hungry, she thought, when he does get home. He's been off on the fell a long time. Still. He'll be all right with Bell. Bell knows every inch up there and it's a fine day. No mist to get lost in.

She opened up one of the parcels she had bought in Penrith market and shook out a flannel nightdress with ribbons and lace, and a long apron of white cotton and a sacking apron to wear over it. "Lovely," she said, parading about. "Museum pieces. Lovely." She put on the white apron which had a pinny top and cross-overs at the back. "Florence Nightingale," she said, twisting before the glass hung in the porch. She tied the sacking apron over it. "Now I'm ready to clean out my chicken-houses," she said.

"Silly," she said next, "playing at being someone else.

Ridiculous. Just as well I'm alone." She began to unpack the rest of the shopping and the grandfather clock struck five.

"I wonder where he is though?" she said and went and stood on the step and stared about. Then she picked up the field-glasses and went and stood in the Home Field. Through the glasses the fells lay as still and empty as they did through her eyes. "Harry," she called. Her voice echoed. She went in and got the bell she used to ring for Harry to come in for meals when he was smaller and played in the beck, just out of sight.

She kept calling and looking and ringing, but nothing happened. She went in and began to wash salad for supper, thinking that the sacking apron was just the thing for cleaning vegetables. She switched on the radio. She made a pudding. She realised that the radio had been telling her for some time the stock market prices in London and the details of the shipping forecast for the next twenty-four hours, and that listening to it she had been thinking all the time about Harry.

She put down the potato peeler and set off up the fell.

I suppose I could have waited till James came in or Robert got back from London. I'm over anxious. I always was a bore about the children. Silly to worry so. She walked along the dry beck strewn everywhere with whitening thistles and climbed up to the top of the bouse where someone seemed to have been digging lately. A lot of earth had fallen into a deep delve in the fell, with turf torn up and the roots of a may tree sticking up at an angle, feeling the fresh air for the first time since Queen Anne was on the throne. A shift, she thought. A land slip. Like when poor old Mr Hewitson got injured. Quite a big one. Maybe it's subsidence in the old mine. She thought of the honeycombs of rocks beneath her feet, and the rocks, hollow like bones, leading to underground rivers and ball-rooms and cathedrals below, and shuddered. The one thing I'd regret about us coming up here would be if any of them ever took up pot-holing.

She thought for a moment that she heard voices, and stopped. Then she thought she heard a faint metallic hammering noise, very thin and distant. "Kendal says it's haunted up here," she said, and hurried on, and up to the top of the fell where you could see in all directions, right to the Nine Standards, the huge old stones that watched from the horizon.

She stood in the long white apron, shading her eyes.

"Wake up," said Bell, "wake up Harry lad. Here. We've got to yell again."

Harry stirred but didn't wake. Bell shook him. "Here. Harry. It's late. It must be about night. They'll be looking by now. There's sense yelling now. More sense than before when they was all away."

"My throat's sore."

"It'll be sorer if we're here all night. It's going to get right cold soon. This place has never seen the sun in a million years."

They were behind the iron-barred grille at the entrance to the mine, peering out in to the cave beyond it over the rubbish and rubble of the sixty years since the bars had been fixed. The outer cave mouth was a maddening ten feet away from the inner, barred opening. From the cave mouth the bouse fell steeply away so that you could see the light beyond beginning to change to shadow as it drew to evening. To Bell and Harry it seemed near midnight.

"We ought to start bashing again, too."

"The tin cans and that are wore out."

"There's the pick and shovel. Come on."

Bell began a great assault on the thick iron bars.

"It's killing me ears," said Harry.

"Get to work with that shovel."

Harry made some lesser noises with the shovel. Then they

61

both stopped and cried "Help" for a while.

Then they sat down again and stared at the bars. Ater a while Harry said, "We'll likely die."

"Get away," said Bell. But dismally. His face was streaked with dirt. It looked gaunt. He kicked the bars with his foot. "By God," he said. "I'se sorry for animals."

"Animals? Sheep could get out. They could ease their way out if they ever wandered in. Dogs could get out. Rabbits could get out. Hares could get out."

"I mean gorillas. Lions and tigers."

"Foxes could get out. Ferrets could get out."

"I mean zoo animals. Caged up. We're caged up. We're caged up like slaves or gorillas. I'll never go near a zoo again."

"Snakes could get out." Harry picked up the end of a chain which hung from the wagon behind him. Already they had tried to heave at the wagons to make them roll up against the iron bars and break the grille down; but it meant pushing up-hill and they were anyway afraid that they might block the entrance altogether and bring down everything. "I'd say we were going to die," Harry said again. He began to feed the chain through the bars. After a bit he had to help it along by jabbing it with the shovel, pushing the shovel sideways through the bars and holding tight to the other end.

"Have you read *Huckleberry Finn*?" asked Bell.

"No."

"Just as well. What you doing?"

"Watching the chain being a snake. Why is it just as well?"

"There was a place like this in *Huckleberry Finn*. Some kids got lost in caves. When they got themselves out – miles away back from the place they'd started, everyone thought they was dead. So all their families blocked up the proper entrance so no other kids could go in again."

"Well I don't wonder at that," said Harry, pressing his

face in to the bars and jabbing on at the chain with the shovel end, urging it down the slope towards the cave mouth.

"No, but there was someone else left inside. A terrible Indian. Ages later when someone went up to have another look around, there was this dead skeleton lying, stretching out its poor bony hands. Horrible."

Harry stretched his hands, and his arms, out to their furthest extent through the bars and forced the chain forward a few more links. "Dead skeleton," he said. "That's not so bad. It's live skeletons I don't like."

"Aye. Think of his last hours."

"D'you think these are our last hours?"

"If we don't get clanking and shouting again they are. Go on. Get clanking that shovel against the bars again. Gis hold of the pick and I'll have a thrust at that chain."

After the morning's thistling Old Hewitson had gone off down Quarry Hill with his scythe over his shoulder like Old Father Time, and James alongside. They waited a while on the wooden bridge in the village for Kendal the sweep. When Kendal's land-rover appeared Old Hewitson, James and the scythe were all installed in it and the land-rover turned and made for a remote farmhouse on Stainmore where propped against the yard wall there stood a large brass bed.

The two ends of the bed and the metal base had been lifted in to the land-rover and then everyone had gone in to the farm house for tea.

This had taken a very long time, for there was a lot to talk about – there is always more to talk about in places where not much seems to happen – and the farmer and his wife did not set them over the yard to the land-rover again to say good-bye and thank them for taking the bed off their hands until after five o'clock.

Then there had to be another long talk from the steering wheel and by the time they eventually rattled off and reached the village, it was time for the stock market prices and the shipping forecast had they been interested in either.

Through the village they went and up Quarry Hill past Light Trees and as far as the culvert bridge over the dry beck.

"Now's the problem," said Kendal, "how to get the bed up the fell."

"I thistled this place this morning," said Old Hewitson. "We might see if it'll run along the beck bottom."

The land-rover lumbered down the bank and into the stream bed. It took its way along with the two old men now and then hitting their heads on the land-rover roof, and James constantly holding his shin. "Good for the liver," said Kendal.

"Not good for the bed," said Old Hewitson. "It's making music like the Sally Army."

They passed the foot of the bouse, where James's Geology book still lay surveying the evening sky, and turned the corner at the bottom of the cleft and the broken wire fence. They lifted down the bed, removed the old wire from the gap and fastened the bed-ends and the metal base across the dry beck.

"Fits a treat," said Old Hewitson. "Very handsome. No need to mention it to the authorities."

"Last a hundred years," said Kendal, "and very interesting it looks. Just the thing for an Area of Outstanding Natural Beauty. Hello."

"What?"

"Did you hear something?"

They stood. The evening, gentle with the warmth of the long day, smelled of gorse and wild thyme and a hundred miles of clean turf. Through the silence came a faint sound of metal, rhythmically hammering from the top of the bouse, and thin and strange lamenting cries.

At the same moment Mrs Bateman in her long apron paced

in to view and stood mournfully shading her eyes and looking
in to the distance.

James gave a scream and fled, kicking aside his Geology
book and vanishing in to the sunset.

He was closely followed by Kendal who made for the
land-rover, shouting wildly to Old Hewitson to follow him,
and starting the engine.

Only Old Hewitson – and Mrs Bateman – stood their
ground, and only old Hewitson saw something come in to
view in queer jerks at the top of the bouse and watched a
rusty and enormous chain emerge from what looked like the
very earth itself, gather speed, slide lumpily forward, drop
through the air and fall at last at his own uneven feet.

"Turn that car, Kendal," he cried. "Get that James back
here. Mrs Bateman, stay up there on the bouse. We're in for
a hard evening. It's going to take the lot of us."

"And for my part," said Mr Teesdale at past ten o'clock at
night, "I'd a mind to leave them there."

"And mine," said Mr Bateman in his London suit which
was not looking its best.

"Sitting there like two fond monkeys. Deserved nuts and
water for a week."

"Beyond me. Beyond me," said Mr Bateman.

"I just couldn't believe – I couldn't believe it," said Mrs
Bateman. "All I did was appear and everyone screamed and
scattered. Ghost! Do I look like a ghost?"

"Yes," said Eileen, Bell's sister, "you did. I seed it once. I
seed that ghost when I was just about to be a teen-ager. Just
before you're teen-age you see ghosts easiest. I read it in a
magazine. Just before you're teen-age you're very psychic
and impressionable."

"I'd give Bell psychic and impressionable," said his father.

"I'd not call that Kendal teen-age," said Mrs Bateman, "at
least not in years."

"I saw no ghosts," said Bell, "I was that busy getting us out."

"Getting us out?" said Harry. "You was going on about dead skeletons and terrible Indians. Who got the chain moving?"

"Aye, well you did. I'll say that."

"A pair of loonies," said James.

"Who went running?" said Harry. "Ghosts of dead miners. Dead miners' mothers! And you a scientist."

"That lad of Meccers never got lost up the mines anyway," said Mrs Teesdale. "I heard tell he took off to South America and got to be a millionaire."

"It was still very dreadful for his mother," said Mr Bateman.

"Tell me when it ever isn't," said Mrs Bateman, collapsed on the Light Trees' sofa, still in her aprons. "Tell me when it ever isn't."

"When they're safe home," said Grandad Hewitson. "Give thanks. They're safe home. And both of them a bit wiser than when the sun rose up this morning."

5 · Granny Crack

The Egg Witch had a mother, a very old woman nobody saw because she lived in bed.

She had been in bed for years. There was nothing at all wrong with her, but one day she just didn't get up. The Egg Witch and the Egg Witch's children and sometimes even the Egg Witch's wispy husband, who spent as much time as possible out of doors on his farm, began to carry up trays. Nightdresses of ancient design appeared upon the Egg Witch's clothes line but that was the only outward sign of Granny Crack. When anyone asked after Granny Crack, the Egg Witch's mother, she just said "Nicely thank you." Or nothing, and glared. They had always been a glaring sort of family, the Cracks.

The Egg Witch had been a Crack, Mrs Teesdale told Mrs Bateman, before she had married. Yorkshire people and we know what *that* means.

"No," said Mrs Bateman.

"They tell you nothing, Yorkshire people, they're not like here."

"But Yorkshire is hardly ten miles away over the fell."

"They're different folk."

Now it happened that Harry had become a friend of the Egg Witch. All those years ago, before he was even school-age and had trampled eggs in to her front path and run off, he had been made to go back next day and say he was sorry. His father had gone with him but had waited at the gate.

Harry had knocked on the Egg Witch's black door and been told through it to go round to the back. His father had watched him depart and return with an enormous bucket and with the scrubbing brush they had brought with them. He had settled down to scrub the path which was as white as snow already, having been scrubbed clean some hours before at the first possible minute after Sunday, when work is wicked. He had scrubbed the clean slabs all the way from the gate back up to the front door, making everything rather puddly. His father had settled down outside the gate with his back to the wall and a book to read.

As Harry reached the front door, wiggling backwards on his knees, it had opened behind him and there had stood the Egg Witch with an apple in her hand. She looked at the path and then at Harry. "It'll do," she said and handed him the apple.

That the Egg Witch had given somebody a present had been talked about in the village for quite some time.

Later Harry's mother had met the Egg Witch in Market Street shopping, and nodded. The next summer when the Egg Witch was out in her garden digging a huge trench for potatoes, Harry and his mother went by and she straightened herself up and glared and said, "Are you comin' in?"

After that they looked in often and sat in the Egg Witch's kitchen (they never went in to the awful parlour again) for a cup of tea, and on one occasion Harry's mother mentioned mothers – and then the flood gates opened.

"Seven years," said the Egg Witch, "seven years she's been up there. The doctor comes and looks to her every now and then. Says she's right as a ninepence. Just given in, that's what she's done. Worked all her life – up before five every morning, milking fifty years, never a holiday all her life. Right away up on Kisdon we lived, miles from nowhere. Made her own butter and cheese and bread. Fed the nine of us out of twenty-five shilling a week – my father was a pig-killer till he died, going round the farms killing and helping here and there hay-times, as we did, us and mother too, carrying pots of stew on harnesses on our backs away up the fell. Such a cook she was! She'd fill a big black pot – one of them with bright, thick silver insides – with potatoes and onions and carrots and a bone, and cover it with water and boil it up slow. Beautiful. Every day oft' week, and bread and syrup for supper. Sundays there'd may be a spare rib pie. Proper spare rib, not this so called spare rib now. And a crust over it. She could heft the sheep and clip the sheep and dip. She could salt the pig and make the sausage and the black puddings. She could stack a rick of hay and corn and she could paint a house inside and out and mend the great roof tiles. She could milk and separate and calve a cow. She never had a day's sickness in her life, no more had we. We never saw a doctor. She had us out of our beds six o'clock each day including Sunday, and she was always last to bed at night. And look at her now."

"Doesn't she even want to talk to anyone?"

"No. She does not."

"Doesn't she read or listen to the wireless?"

"No. She does not. She lies there night and day looking at the ceiling. Night and day, winter and summer, these seven years."

"Whatever can have set it off?"

"We don't know. She'd been down here living with me for a bit when it happened. Mind *I* think I know."

"Oh?"

"It was something on television. Something she saw on the News. It was about the time them Americans went to the moon.

"She's not silly, mind," the Egg Witch added, "she's still sharp. What's more we all know she doesn't stay in bed all the time. We can't catch her at it, but when we're out hay-timing or it's ram sales in Kirkby, or Ravenstonedale or Brough Show and there's no alternatives to leaving her alone, there's signs she gets up to things."

"Up to things?"

"Up to things. However else would she know the colour we'd painted the kitchen? 'Never liked black in a kitchen' she said the other day. *We* never told her. No – she'd been down."

"What would happen if you just carried her downstairs and put her in the car and took her for a drive?"

"Oh – she'd create. She'd take a stroke after all this time, the doctor says. It'd be murder. It's the countryside she's turned against you see. It's the land she hates. She hates it. She's had enough – all them long Swaledale winters, all that scratting and scraping and never in all her life seeing anywhere more than ten-twelve miles from her home. She hates anyone that's a traveller. She always was venomous with the gypsies – there was never a gypsy dared come anywhere near Kisdon. I wouldn't take you up to see her, Mrs Bateman. She's still got a very bitter tongue. I wouldn't trust her to see a Londoner. It's what got in to her that morning we switched on the moon and saw them men in their siren suits bobbing about."

"I suppose," said Mrs Bateman, "that she has really gone – well, a little bit off her head. In London they would take her in to hospital now and then – just to give you a break."

70

"That I will *not* have," said the Egg Witch, all her whiskers bristling. "I know my duty."

Just before the Batemans left at the end of summer there was a great blackberry picking going on in the Hollow Land. It was a wonderful blackberry year and everywhere you could see people patiently picking in the lanes with plastic bags and bowls and even buckets. The best place for a bramble as everybody knew was the Egg Witch's lane and they went there first as soon as the berries had ripened. Harry had been sent out to get some to take home to London. He got a lift down with Mr Teesdale on the tractor to Teesdale's farm and then walked the rest.

But he was too late. The bushes were bare.

He thought that he would walk on to the Egg Witch's and ask if she knew anywhere else there'd be some, down behind Blue Barns in the woods perhaps.

When he got to Blue Barns he was puzzled because everything was so quiet. It was as quiet as on the first frightening Sunday he had called there for eggs long ago. The yard and the garden were quite empty – even the kennel was empty. The whole farm stood sunbathing in peaceful early autumn light – rose-hips by the gate, bright dahlias in the borders, healthy bright potato flowers, and two or three swallows sitting on a wire warm as toast and wondering if there was any point in going to Africa.

Harry went round the back and opened the kitchen door and called hello, as he always did now. He met complete silence. He looked in the rooms and they were empty. The kitchen fire was laid but not lit and there was an extra neatness about the table and the sink and draining board that meant nobody had been there for some time. Harry remembered all at once the Show at Brough, where Bell and everyone had gone and where Mr Teesdale had been hurrying to on the tractor. The kennel was empty because of the sheep dog trials. They'd be hours getting back – sheep dog trials being as long as it takes. And then all the judging of the plants and cakes and rum-butters.

Never mind, he'd just go home. He didn't like the feel of Blue Barns without the Egg Witch in it, and that was odd when he remembered how frightened of her he used to be. The house had a different quiet about it without her. Even a quiet house has some little noises in it if you listen – ticks and creaks, a hum from a fridge or a flap from a curtain or a squeak from a board. Today Blue Barns was so quiet it was like somebody holding his breath and listening for himself.

Harry thought of the old lady all alone upstairs and prickles walked across the back of his neck. I'm off, he thought.

And there was a tremendous and horrendous crash from just behind his head!

He was half way down the yard, beyond the pump before he stopped running.

Then he listened. "I can't," he said – and very slowly set off back.

The kitchen had become completely still again but from under the dairy door there trickled a stream of what looked like blood.

This time he ran out of the door over the yard past the kennel, past the silos and a good way down the bramble lane.

Then he stopped again.

He'd have to go back.

If there had been anyone about he need not have gone back. If there were anybody at home in any of the farms along by the village he could have run in to one and told them and left it at that. But everyone would be at the Show.

Maybe he could telephone the police? He could telephone his father and mother packing up at Light Trees. He could reverse the charges since he had no money – or just dial 999.

Except there wasn't a telephone box.

But there was a telephone – back in the kitchen of Blue Barns. The kitchen with blood pouring out under the dairy door.

Harry walked slowly back, up the lane past the silos, past the kennel, past the pump and in to the kitchen where a very old lady in a long frilly white dress was standing eating a slice of bread and drinking blackberry juice out of a jam jar.

She was very, very small with a sharp face, the chin turning up to meet the nose that turned down. Her jaw was going round and round in a circle and her eyes were in two round shadowy caves but you could still see they were bright, bright blue. Her hair was white and puffy and thin and all over the place.

Behind her through the now open dairy door Harry could see a great ocean of blackberry juice flowing all over the dairy floor. Small purple dabs walked out of it up to where the old lady stood. She didn't look frightening at all. Rather frightened if anything.

She said in a tiny voice, like a flute down inside her, "It might have been the cat."

"There is no cat," said Harry. "Leastways it's not about. It'll be off somewhere. You can't say it was the cat – and the door left shut no doubt."

"Maybe," she said, "it was the gypsies. The gypsies got in."

"Gypsies don't come spilling juice."

"Gypsies does anything," said the flute.

Harry looked in the dairy. The juice flowed from a big broken bowl. Above the bowl, from a hook in the ceiling was a muslin bag of dry brambles that had been dripping all night. It was a large bag that must have dripped out juice in pints, the pints now flowing free. "I'm not clearing that up," said Harry. "I'm always clearing things up here."

The old woman looked very sad.

"She'll go at me."

"I don't wonder." Harry looked about for a cloth, then he said, "No – I'm *not* cleaning it all up."

Granny Crack took a bite of the bread and a drink from the jar, daintily like a swallow. "You're Harry," she said, "Harry Bateman. I've seen you before."

"I've not seen you."

"I've seen you through upstairs windows. I'm light-footed." She looked down at her pale little marbly feet with a purple rim to them and said, "I'll to my bed."

"You'll leave a trail."

"I'll wash my feet."

"*Where* will you wash your feet?"

The old woman looked perplexed.

"I'm not washing your feet here," said Harry, "not in that sink. You can't climb on that draining board. You'll have to wash them in the trough in the yard."

"I'll not go outside. I don't go outside."

"Or there's a tap for her dahlias in the front garden."

"It's outside."

"I'll not clear up for you if you don't wash your feet."

"Oh!" came out of the flute, long and wailing and thin.

"I'm glad my gran's not like you," said Harry. He found a cloth and mopped up juice with a very bad grace. "The flags'll need scrubbing," he said, "and the lino's stained for ever. And the bowl's done for."

"Throw it," said Granny Crack.

"*Throw?*"

"Throw it int' midden and cover it."

"I'll throw it," said Harry, "if you'll come out in the garden and have your feet washed at that tap."

"Kill me," she said. "You want to kill me."

But when Harry had thrown the broken bowl away on the midden she trotted after him in to the front garden and stood quite interestedly with her feet under the tap. He turned it on and the flute laughed. "Like Castle Beck," she said.

"Gives you the jumps." Then she skipped off and wiped her feet all over the grass right down to the garden gate.

"I'm off now," said Harry. "You'll be all right." He opened the gate.

Granny Crack trotted after him in her white nightie.

"Hey – you can't come with me. Go back," he said, feeling he'd got landed with some sort of crazy, disobedient dog.

Granny Crack grinned and sat down by the gate with her back to the wall where Mr Bateman had sat to read his book. The September sun shone down on her and she turned her smooth face up to it and munched with her small mouth at nothing for a time. She twiddled her lilac coloured feet and let the sun warm them on the warm bank.

"You're a boy," she said. "I had boys. They went off. There wasn't enough for them. You're not from these parts."

"Some of the time I am," said Harry. "Off and on I've been here for ages. We live in London mostly though."

"London," said Granny Crack, "I never saw London Town."

"It's all right," said Harry. "Up here's better. More seems to go on up here."

She turned her head to him. Every bone in it could be seen through the wispy white hair and her mouth fell open in a little O. Her blue eyes stared in great surprise.

"More goes on," the distant flute said. It was difficult, Harry thought, to know what feelings started the words off, for the voice had no expression in it. It was a voice just taken out for use after being long put away.

"I'd like once to have seen London Town."

Harry found that he was trying to tell her. He was not much of a talker and never had been, but once he got going he found it easy – she looked at him with such wide eyes he might have been telling her adventures. Yet it was only the zoo and the Tower and Buckingham Palace and Nelson's Column and all the old boring things you take visitors to. He told her biking on the Common was best – but nothing like biking here. And you never noticed weather hardly, or trees and so on. There was drunks, of course, to look at on Waterloo station and painters hanging their pictures on Hyde Park railings on Sunday mornings, and the lights over the bridges coming back late after the pantomime at Christmas. No excitements much though –

He droned on and on. After a time Granny Crack turned her queer old face from him and seemed to be smiling. She turned her face up to the white crescent of the day-time moon. And Harry droned.

The Egg Witch found the pair of them sitting there, contented in the sunshine.

6 · The Icicle Ride

"Can Harry come out?" asked Bell bobbing up at Light Trees' kitchen window and making Harry's mother drop a pan. She had been standing at the sink dreaming out over the snow-covered view to see if she could sight Helvellyn and the Saddleback sparkling against the sky.

"Heavens, Bell, wherever did you spring from? Only sheep look in on me at this sink."

"I come over the stile. You could have seen me all across the field. I were watchin' you."

"You might have waved, Bell."

"I waved and I called but you were busy over me head looking at the snow."

"I can see your footmarks now. Come round quick. I can't stand shouting here and it's too cold to open the window."

"Harry," she called.

Bell came round in to the house and stamped his feet in the stone porch and then took his boots off and came in to the living room and stamped a bit more in his socks and got in near the fire with the long green furry branches sticking out two feet in to the room. He came right in to the house now without knocking. He was long past knocking, for the holiday folks had been here now for years.

Bell was much bigger than at the first angry hay-time, though he still wore the same bobble hat he'd worn then, with a piece of his hair coming out of the top. His face hadn't altered. Neither had Harry altered much. He was stretched out upstairs making a railway train out of playing cards that ran across the little bedrooms and over the landing and up the step to the bathroom in rather the style of the Trans-Siberian Express. He encouraged this train by singing to it.

Sometimes when the song grew louder and the train had a long incline to go up there would be a roar from the little room at the back of the house where his father was writing for the newspapers about important things which had little to do with playing-card trains.

"Hush as you go up," said Harry's mother to Bell, "Mr Bateman's got a deadline."

Harry had a dead line too. All the carriages had spilled about all over the place and Harry was lying on the floor on his back among them looking up through the landing window at the high line of fell with no cow or sheep standing out along the sharp line of it like black cut-outs, which he liked to see.

"There's no cows and no sheep out," he said to Bell.

"And no rabbits and no nothing else," said Bell. "By, but it's freezing. D'you want to come an icicle ride?"

"Yes," said Harry getting up and putting on a jersey. "What is it?"

"You'll see. Are you ready? You'll need some good fist-covers. And a hat."

"There's plenty downstairs with my zip jacket."

"Int' porch?" said Bell throwing a second jersey at him.

78

"'ere, get this on an' all."

"Yes, int' porch," said Harry.

"In *the* porch," said his mother appearing from the kitchen. "Now whatever's happening? Dinner's ready in five minutes and it's a good stew."

"Bell wants me to go a niceicle ride."

"A nice little ride! A day like this! What are you thinking of then, Bell – a central-heated Bentley?"

"No, an icicle ride, Mrs Bateman."

"But will Harry's track-bike keep the road?"

"Oh I'd think so. It's not a real rough track-bike. It's got brakes. I've only got Mam's sit-up-and-beg and the roads down the bottom are gritted."

"It seems a funny day for bike rides."

"It's just up here on the fell it's so fierce," said Bell. "Down the bottom they're all out doing their shopping."

"Well, stay for your dinner with us first," said Mrs Bateman, "and I'll ring your mother. Then Mr Bateman will take you both and the bike down when he goes to catch his deadline at the post-office. Will the post-office be a good starting place?"

"Grand. We're going down Castledale."

"Oh well, that's a nice level road for a mile or so if you're wrapped up and there'll be nothing about to skid in to you today. There's a phone box at Hell Gill. You can ring from there if you want lifting back. You're sure now it won't be iced over?"

"I'd think not," said Bell. "We can always get off and walk if it is."

"And you've asked at home?"

"WHAH, YARRAH, WHAH," came from the top of the stairs they were talking on. "However am I going to get this done in time for the post – ?" so that Bell was saved the difficulty of replying.

They picked up Bell's bike from the back shed of the Teesdales' farm as they passed, seeing no one. Snow was very thick on Bell's father's fields and the roofs of his buildings and up against the front door that was never used in winter. Bell's family was round the back, his father doing his tax, his mother baking, his grandad making mole traps and his sister Eileen in bed with a magazine and nobody heard them call. At the post-office they were just in time to see the post-van driving away towards the Oxenholm road to the train, and had quite an exciting time chasing it with Harry's father's piece of writing which, when they had flashed and tooted long enough the postman noticed and said he would see arrived at London for the deadline. Then they returned to the post-office and Mr Bateman helped them out with the bikes and watched them off under a sky grown very low and dark towards Nateby; but you could see from his face that he was still mostly inside the envelope he had just handed in to the van. The two boys were just shadows passing away from him.

"You did say an icicle ride?" said Harry, pedalling fast to keep up with the large wheels of the sit-up-and-beg. "I'd not really want a *bicycle* ride today. Whoops!"

The track-bike did a glorious swan-lake across the thick packed snow of the road and Harry slid off and landed underneath it. The grit was over the snow, but it was beginning to get a glaze over it.

"It's a bicycle ride int' first place but the main event's an icicle ride all right," said Bell, "or we'll hope it is. It may not come to anything. Often it doesn't but once it did."

"Did what?"

"Come to something. To icicles. If you know what you're on about looking."

"Like blackberrying?"

"That's it. Wow!" This time it was Bell's bike's turn to do a graceful John Curry and Bell trying to catch up with it before it hit the cattle grid. They both paused for breath and looked down at Wateryat Bottom and the frozen-over river there. The flat plain like a green, sheep-nibbled psalm of a place in summer, looked today like somewhere that had come grinding down from Alaska. Two dismal gypsy caravans stood on it and one sorrowful-looking gypsy pony. Had it not been for the pony you'd have said no living creature had anything to do with the caravans. They were shuttered in, tight curtained, and the rubbish around them had been made to look quite ancient and respectable like ruins under its fat layer of snow.

"How far is an icicle ride?" said Harry. The sunshine of the morning had now completely gone and it was very grey light.

"A mile or two as far as I remember. Not much more anyway. We'll ride on a bit. Then if it gets rough we'll push. It's fine and frosty all right. Help!" A land-rover suddenly appeared round a corner and fainted across the road nearly in to the stone wall when it caught sight of them. A head looked out. It was a farmer Bell knew who lived at the far end of Castledale. His land-rover was solid with sheep he'd found straying and was taking to Nateby pound. A wall of yellow-eyed wool looked out over his shoulders. The sheep's eyes rolled about and the farmer's eyes rolled about, too.

"Whatever's this then? Goin' off youth 'ostelling?"

"Just a bit ride," said Bell.

"Yer father know?"

"Yes," said Harry.

"Then he's dafter than I thought," said the farmer revving and shuddering at the gears, and, all the sheep a-tremble, he passed them by. It seemed very cold and silent in the dale when the noise of the engine had gone.

"Come on," said Bell. Totteringly up they got and pedalled safely for quite a long way in the more sheltered bends beyond Pendragon Castle, bumpity bump by the holiday cottages, bolted and barred like the gypsy caravans.

"You're the only incomers comes in winter," said Bell. "Folks say London must be a pretty terrible place if you prefer up here this weather."

"London's not bad," said Harry, and the bike took a header for a small ravine, "but it's not exciting."

When they'd gathered up the bike this time and looked it over, Bell thought it might be an idea for Harry to finish the icicle ride on foot. It wasn't that the track-bike was finished altogether, but the brakes when you squeezed them seemed to swing about rather. In fact as Bell squeezed one of them, it came off in his hand.

"Put the thing int' road side," said Bell, "it likely won't get stolen this weather." They propped it up against the wall where it leaned looking rather relieved, like the dying Indian in the poem, said Bell.

"What poem?"

"Poem at school. About a dying Indian. When they get ill, Red Indians, and they're crossing the prairie, they just has to be left. Somebody else takes over their kids and that and they just watch as the tribe goes walking off in to the distance. And then they die. It's like *The Guns of Navarone*."

"I didn't like *The Guns of Navarone*," said Harry, "though they didn't actually leave him. My father didn't like it either. He said it was daft. War's daft."

"This poem wasn't daft," said Bell. "It was 'orrible. All of them leaving her lying there and the baby looking back. All the vultures watching."

"There'll be hospitals now," said Harry. "I hope the vultures don't get after my bike."

"I'd like to see a vulture out on a day like this."

They tramped on, Harry trotting behind the sit-up-and-beg. He enjoyed trotting. It kept his hands warmer than the track-bike. He watched his breath puffing and then began to move his fists like pistons. Soon he began to sing.

The Icicle Ride

"Give over that," said Bell, "it's all we need."

On they went – past the chapel, past the dark-windowed prim-looking old school house long since shut down, past the house where an old woman used to keep goats in her front sitting room among the furniture, past the little lane that led to the oldest of all the fell cottages in the dale.

"Used to be vampires up yonder. In one of them cottages," said Bell, "Leastways I think it was them. It was somewhere. Anyway there's one buried in Dent churchyard."

Puff, puff, puff, went Harry.

"Got a stake through his heart and a chain up through the coffin, the end of it sticking out and fastened with a ring into his gravestone. To hold him down."

Puff, puff, puff.

"See he don't wander and POUNCE on folks."

Puff, puff.

"Ain't you interested then? Ain't you flait at all, Harry? You're a right puzzle."

Harry said nothing for a bit and they turned into the great black cave of the railway bridge and out from under it again and past a farm gate with a kennel but no dogs to shout at them. "It's cold if Eddie Cleesby's took his dog in," said Bell.

"Were they thinking he'd be hungry yet?" said Harry.

"Whichways?"

"Yon vampire in Dent church yard."

"You'd best not let your mother hear you saying 'yon'. Or 'hungry yet'. You say 'hungry still'."

"Hungry still. I'd see he'd be still if he was dead. But why'd he be hungry?"

"Never said he'd be hungry."

"You said they put a steak in his heart."

"A *stake*. Aye. A great splinter."

"Oh I thowt as you meant juicy with onions."

"*Thowt!*" said Bell. "Speak right, can't yer. You'll finish up a savage."

Under the great shadow of Wild Boar Fell they went and Bell decided he'd leave his bicycle for the vultures, too. "We'll walk next bit. It's not owt now. 'Ere – throw yer arms about yerself backwards and forwards. That way yer fingers'll come back on you. We'll need 'em shortly."

"For icicles?"

"Wait on and ye'll see."

But though they walked and walked, Harry saw nothing special – nothing more than the lonely road and the sweeping snowy fells and the lowering head of the Wild Boar rock above them. A beck they came on was as deep with snow as any dry land and only known to be there by a faint musical tinkling like bells.

"Them's the fairies," said Bell. "Folks had to make up something before the telly."

"Mr Hewitson's seen the fairies," said Harry, "he tellt' me."

"*Told* thee. What – our grandad? Old Hewitson? You tek no account of what he says. He's no better'n Kendal the sweep.

"Mind," he added, "I know he says he did. And his gran did too. Smearing butter over gateposts they was. Over Ladthwaite. Wonder whatever sort of good that did a body."

"A body?"

"Anybody."

"Bell."

"Aye?"

"Bell – where's the icicle ride?"

"Not far now."

They turned a little off the road, full in to the teeth of a piercing wind coming down to meet them off Mallerstang Edge. "Somewhere very close."

But he had begun to look serious.

The Icicle Ride

"Bell?"

"Aye?"

"Bell – where is it we're going? Bell – I'se tired."

"*I'm* tired. *I'm* tired."

"Well, if you're tired, too –"

"No I'se not tired. I's just telling thee to speak right or your mother'll stop you coming out."

"No, she'll never. Bell . . . *Bell!*" – for Bell had disappeared now off the road and over a wall. Harry heard his feet go thump, scrunch in to a great heap of snow beyond. Then there was quiet.

"*Bell,*" roared Harry and felt how his feet had gone away, and looked at his fingers, all blue when he took off his glove, and how his face was sharp and stingy and his ears ached and burned at the same time and the wind blew at him, sharp as stakes in the heart. "*Bell,* I want to go *back.*"

And then three things happened. The wind dropped, Bell's round face reappeared smiling over the wall, and the sun came suddenly beaming and gleaming from under the lowest and blackest of the dismal clouds to take a last look at the short and bitter day. Long, yellow brilliant rays broke across Castledale and for miles and miles and miles snow glittered like a million tons of diamonds. The little black snow-posts to mark the fell tracks stuck up like barbed wire spikes with blue shadows behind them, sharp as arithmetic. "Come ower this now," said Bell, "and see if it's been worth it."

And Harry climbed up the steps of stone in the wall and put his miserable blue hands in the sopped gloves on top of it and dropped down into the scrunching snow – and deeper than Bell, being smaller, nearly to his waist.

And there round a corner to the left where the beck fell sheer, stood high as the sky a chandelier of icicles. Hundreds upon hundreds upon hundreds of them down the shale steps of a waterfall. There were long ones and short ones and middling ones and fat ones like an arm and thin ones like a thread. They hung down from up as high as you could see and down to your very wellingtons. And not only water had turned to spears of glass but every living thing about – the grasses, the rushes, the spider webs, the tall great fearless thistles. You could pull the tubes of ice off the long wands of the loose-strife. You could lift them off like hollow needles. You could look right down them like crystal test tubes. You could watch them twist like fairy ear-rings. And as the sun reached them they all turned at once to every colour ever known – rose and orange and blue and green and lilac – and Harry and Bell watched them until the sun slipped down a little and left them icicles again.

"It don't happen often," Bell said. "Once before I seed it when Grandad brought me years back – your age. It happens when there's a temperature change – very quick. Snap-snap. It freezes sudden. Turns them all to ice in midflow. All the grasses an all – just as they're standing or bending."

"Just like a spell. Like *The Snow Queen*."

They stood on.

"Can we pick some?"

They began to pick. Not very bravely at first. It seemed a sin to spoil it. "But it'll all be gone tomorrow," said Bell. "Grandad says they don't often last a day."

They took the tips off the rushes and pulled. They broke off the water icicles like peppermint rock or toffee. They took all thicknesses and laid them carefully in the snow. Somewhere they found in a pocket some bits of John Robert twine to bind them and parcelled together a heap of the thickest. Then Harry collected some of the very fine threads in to his hands and they slowly climbed over the wall and walked, not feeling the cold at all back down the road.

It was growing quite dark now but the road was shiny enough to follow. When they reached Bell's bike, they fastened his sheaf at the back across his panniers where they stuck out at either side like glass firewood. Harry walked in front, carrying his delicate bundle upright like a bouquet. They walked for ages without talking.

"Here's mine," said Harry, looking at the dying Indian track-bike. "But if I push it, what do I do with these? I'd best leave it. My father can fetch it tomorrow. It's no good without brakes and there'll be nobody much passing to pinch it. I want to get these home safe. I'd like my mother to see them."

"Aye – I want Grandad to get a look at mine," said Bell, "and we'll have to look sharp for it's warmer."

"Funny to get warmer when the sun's gone down," said Bell, "but it's been a funny day altogether. Magic rather like as if there's something watching.

"It *is* warmer," said Bell later. They had passed Wild Boar, the railway bridge and the empty dog kennel, the school and the chapel, all dead and dark. "It must be because it's snowing a bit."

By Outhgill village it was snowing a lot. There was a light here and a light there in the looming dark. Bell knew someone at the shop, which wasn't that far off if he could find it, he said. But then – the icicles. If they stopped now they wouldn't get them home. Already they had a more slithery, softer sort of feel – like the road ahead.

"We'll press on," he said.

"My mother said to ring from Hell Gill phone box. Where's Hell Gill phone box, Bell?"

"I think we've passed it," said Bell. "Come on. We're getting on. We've passed the place where she kept her goats and we're nearly at the chapel."

"We're way past the chapel," said Harry, "and the school."

"Are we? I'm getting muddled."

"Well, I seed a building."

"Saw – "

"Saw a – Bell, I think we ought to go back. To the shop at Outhgill. It's snowing like feathers."

They turned to go back, gasping a bit in to the snow and found that the lights of the few cottages at Outhgill had disappeared. The night had fallen and the snow fluttered steadily and softly and determinedly down, silencing the whole world.

"This dale were cut off for six weeks in 1947," said Bell. "My dad couldn't go to school, all that time. Till Easter. They kept putting this place ont' wireless – aerial photographs in the newspapers and prayers in churches."

They rounded a bend, very slowly and stood completely still – for the road was not there. Instead of it, a great sweeping drift of snow flowed across before them and looped up to the wall. But the wall had gone, too. As they stood, wiping over their faces every minute and peering at the drift, it grew dimmer and dimmer and the feathers flew so fast you could scarcely see between them.

"Well, they'll come for us," said Bell. "They'll probably be on their way. From Nateby. They'll have started."

"Yes. If they can get through," said Harry.

"Aye, if they can get through."

A worse sort of cold had started to grow inside Harry and his legs which had until now been stiff and numb felt loose and floppy. "What shall we do, Bell?"

"Do? Well –" He felt very much older than Harry as Harry asked him. At the same time he felt very young indeed. He peered in to the dark and his legs, too, began to feel odd. Then he said, "I think I can see a light."

"Where?"

"Over there. Look. A lil'e flicker."

"I can't see it."

"I can. Come on. Over off t' road. Hold to the bike to keep together. Come on now and push. Fetch over here now away from that drift."

The bike, with them behind it, careered over a hump and began to slide fast down a smooth snow slope to the level ground. Harry saw a light, too, and in a minute both of them heard the tinkle of a little stream which sometimes was the broad river at Wateryat Bottom.

The light grew, and all at once they bumped right up against something – against a head and a juddering, shuddering mass, the clink of a metal wall. A black, wet, hairy, miserable old face peered forward at them and then gave a great sobbing scream.

"It's a pony," said Bell in a voice that might have said, It's God's own favourite guardian angel. "It's a pony tied up. It's the gypsies."

Then the dogs began – perhaps half a dozen of them by the racket, turning both vans to sounding boxes. "Shout," said Bell. "Shout above them or they'll eat us."

They both yelled and beat at the van side. Hysterical barks of dogs answered.

Nothing happened otherwise.

"They're not in," said Harry beginning to cry. "They're not answering. We'll die."

"Git yelling," said Bell, and again they roared and thumped. "They wouldn't leave lights on for dogs."

"It's maybe ghosts," said Harry. "Or magic. We can't get to them like the Hand of Glory. We might be meant to throw milk ower or something." He sat down and crawled under the van putting the icicle bouquet at a distance right under the van wheels.

"*Yell*, will yer," said Bell, "and don't talk so fancy."

They yelled again and from above them at last there was a slow bumping and thumping noise and a groaning, grumbling sort of voice. They were human words, though they didn't sound very welcoming. They rose to a shout and the dogs were quieter for a moment. Then steps could be heard by Harry above his head and a fumbling and scraping at the door beside Bell's ear. "Yell again," cried Bell – and the barks and snarls and grunts from inside mingled with their own high shouts.

And other shouts.

And toots.

And furious noises.

Through the snow, coming down across the Wateryat behind them there was a dark cluster moving, with a light. With several torches. "Hi!" the cluster was calling, "Bell there? Harry? Are you there?"

In a swirl there was Mr Teesdale and Mr Bateman and James Bateman and another man, and in ten shakes Bell and Harry were scooped away and trudged off with and dumped down in the back of the Teesdales' land-rover. Then with huge revvings and roarings and performances, the land-rover turned on what it hoped was the road. Mr Teesdale stuck his head out and shouted at the other man, who was the farmer who had seen them setting off in his van full of lost sheep. "Are you right then, Sedge?" asked Teesdale. "Are you going to risk going on?"

"Aye, I'm right. I'll risk it."

"Thanks then. Goodnight."

The farmer went on up Castledale in to the snow and the Teesdale land-rover turned back towards Nateby and Teesdales and Light Trees. At Bell's farm, Bell was hustled out and his mother's voice could be heard as the back door opened, uplifted like the gypsy dogs.

"We'll have a go getting up Quarry Hill," said Mr Teesdale. "They'll both be best in their own beds. If the snow goes forward you're like to be all cut off, the lot of you, up there, so you may as well all be together."

"I'm afraid," said Mr Bateman, "we're nothing but a nuisance to you. We should have stayed at home for Christmas – in London where we belong."

"It's not you I blame," said Mr Teesdale. "You could

know no better. It's that lad of mine. Off down Castledale with hard frost and snow and ice, and on bikes. By Lord, wait till I get hold of that Bell. Let's hope no harm's come to your Harry."

But funnily enough it was Bell who took cold and Harry who was right as ninepence after the icicle ride. The telephone held up between the two houses even though the snow was so deep over the next week that there wasn't a wall to be seen between Birket and the Lake District. News therefore came through about Bell's bronchitis every day and much tutting and exclaiming.

Five days later, when everyone had calmed down a bit and got used to the lie of the land the Light Trees people managed to walk down to see how Bell was – and once they had all exploded in to the Teesdale kitchen the noise of tongues would have put Bedlam to shame.

Harry made his way up to where Bell was still propped up in bed wrapped in blankets and trying to get interested in a pack of cards. He looked glum. "I should of left you droning on at them cards that day instead of us goin' off," he said in a voice that sounded like Jamie the old horse-rake when you tried to move the gears. "I'se to write a letter of thanks to that owd Sedge who tellt' 'em where they'd find us."

"I've had to write one, too," said Harry.

"Feel proper soft."

"I don't."

"You don't?"

"I'm glad we went. We saw the icicles."

"You can't tell them about icicles. Icicles just got melted and gone. We never even got 'em home. I never showed 'em Grandad."

"What's thou never showed Grandad?" said old Hewitson lumping in.

"Icicles."

"You seed them icicles again did you? So that's what it was

all about."

"Lot o' good it did," said grumbling Bell, "no more'n fairies smearing butter on gate-posts ever did."

"Watch thyself now," said old Hewitson. "There's words we use and words we don't use to this day. There's round-about ways of mentioning those people. It's possible to be too direct. Remember that, young Harry. Those people don't like to be called by their name."

"There seems a lot of things it's best to be quiet about," said Harry. "I suppose it's in case you don't get believed."

"Oh *believed* is nothing," said old Hewitson, producing chocolate cornflakes from somewhere. "Getting believed's the least part of it. It's going about and seeing after things as matters. I'se seed them icicles once, you's seed them once. Our Bell's seed them twice. I reckon we're all lucky. It's all that matters – seeing them. In fact maybe if you hadn't set out to see 'em, they wouldn't have been there. We'll never know."

"What's that mean when it's at home?" said Bell.

"Tea's ready," came a shout from downstairs.

"It means as it means. Think of sounds. Does it ever occur to thee, Bell Teesdale, Harry Bateman, that none of the sounds floating about the world wouldn't stand chance, stand *chance*, without ears out ready for 'em? James was talking of it. Sounds need sounding boards of ears. Just think, before there was ears to reverberate off, there was not a sound int' world – not even from oceans (not as I think a great deal of oceans, twice at Morecambe being very much a disappointment to me). And why not? Because sounds go floating about silent until there's an ear for 'em to come up against. Same thing with eyes for all I know. Icicles may need eyes to look at them."

"There's no icicles for eyes to see now," said Harry, watching the big splashing raindrops that had started to turn the yard below Bell's bedroom window to a sloppy black and white pudding. "They're all gone."

"Who's to say they're gone? Think it out. Just think it out. And Harry, come to thy tea. Bell's to look at the playing cards and have a sleep again – but he'll be up for Christmas and you'll be both away on them poor old bikes again."

"Maybe there won't be any bikes. If any eyes fell on them. I'd not be surprised if they weren't there when we go looking for them – and nothing to do with magic."

"Eyes did fall on 'em. A gypsy feller come round with them yesterday wanting reward, which your father gave him and a dozen eggs for luck. He'd had a hard walk through."

"However did he know they were ours?" said Harry.

"I thowt gypsies were nowt but thieves," said Bell.

"He knew," said old Hewitson, "he knew, and thief or no thief, he fetched 'em back. There's ways and means, and some folks' minds catches on in different ways than others. And there's many a thing you can't explain."

7 · The Household Word

If you follow the road on from Light Trees you get to the beck that sometimes runs on top of the ground and sometimes below it. Then, you go on up the hill and turn right before the fell gate and away down the deep rough lane to the low water meadows where the herons stand. Then you come to Dukerdale, and standing at its head the farm called Dark Trees where Tatton and Hannah live. They have lived there a long time, often snowed in for up to six weeks in winter with milk from the one cow tending to freeze in the pail, a fridge full of food if Hannah remembers to fill it, and a television set which quite often works beautifully and which they find a great blessing and wonder however their parents and grandparents did without.

But then at last two or three things brought all to an end. Tatton's rent went sky-high to nearly double and so did the price of feed and hay. Hannah's back began to give trouble and Tatton couldn't dip sheep without her, nor in hay-time could he bale and lift. The terrible winter of '78 froze the pipes for the first time in memory and they had to break ice on the beck. The new lambs froze, too, and the television aerial. The winter went on so long that the deep freeze emptied so that they came to within a packet of fish to being helicoptered – which would have been disgrace.

So they decided to move back to Dentdale where Tatton had been born – 'into a railway family' so he said. That winter – though he'd known bad ones before – set him thinking how silly he was ever to have tried farming at all thirty years ago. It was railways he had in his blood, he said, not sheep. His family had been to do with the main line over Shap since the first wild men from Ireland and Timbuctoo with their coloured hats and their own laws and marriage ceremonies had arrived there, with muscles of steel to build the great fell cut and viaduct a hundred and more years ago.

The more he thought about it, the more sure he was that he had been in the wrong job, and the more he said so, the more depressed he became. He found an old signal box with cottage attached on the single track line over Smardale with a level crossing beside it. The signal man was still living in it but as there hadn't been a train past in fifteen years he was getting mournful. So one mournful man sold to another mournful man and they both cheered up.

What happened to the signal man goodness knows, but Tatton and Hannah were delighted. Arrangements were made for selling the deep freeze – for the signal box was hardly a step from shops. The cow Tatton gave to Bell Teesdale for his own. Such furniture as wouldn't fit – the old oak settles, the meal chest and the big grandfather clock, Hannah said were so cumbersome that whoever came to Dark Trees next was welcome to them.

So when the London family walked across for eggs to Dark Trees one day, they found a great difference in the air. Tatton was singing a Methodist hymn to the cow and

Hannah was writing her will.

"But you're not dying, Hannah, just moving house."

"I'm far from dying," she said. "But I can't move everything from here to yonder and so I'm giving my bequests in advance. That way some people will be in time for 'em as maybe wouldn't be, and what's more, I'll be here to be thanked, which makes people feel square. I know I've times over been shamed when I've been left a keep-sake and no one to write to over it. Now then, these are for you, Mrs Bateman, and this is for young Harry."

"I couldn't, I couldn't," said Mrs Bateman. "Oh thank you," said Harry.

"Just look," they both said when they got back, "there was simply no way of saying no. We've known them such a short time compared to others. Oh, they are kind!"

Everyone gazed at the red and white patchwork quilts and Harry's golden lustre tea-pot.

"We'll put the quilts on the guests' beds this week-end," said Mrs. Bateman. "They don't smoke, do they?"

"I don't know. They might."

"Well, we'll put them on the beds and then if they start smoking downstairs we'll go quickly up and take them off again. What about the tea pot, Harry? Could I put flowers in it in one of the rooms? Will the guests be the sort to notice I wonder?"

"Who are they?" asked Harry.

"Television people coming to talk to your father about work. The lady's famous. Everybody sees her once or twice a week. She's a household word. To do with the News."

"Oh politics," said Harry. "They'll not notice quilts and tea pots."

"Then maybe it's time they had their attention drawn that way," said Mrs Bateman, sounding for a minute – it was happening more and more these days – like a countrywoman.

"There's somebody famous coming," said Harry to Eileen,

Bell's sister, down in Teesdales' kitchen. He drew his finger round Eileen's mixing bowl and licked uncooked gingerbread. "She's on telly. She's a household word."

"Give over," said Eileen, "eating slather!" and hit him with the wooden spoon.

"Give over hitting Harry," said Bell. "You did it yourself times. When you were young. I mind."

"She's on all the big programmes," said Harry. "She's beautiful and clever and she catches them out with questions."

"Oh her," said Eileen.

"What – her?" said Mr Teesdale coming in from sheep. "Well now." He began to wash himself at the sink, all over his face and his arms and his hair and his hands, rubbing the whole mass of him afterwards with a scrap of hard towel. "Coming up to Light Trees is she? Well, we'll all be out to see. It'll be red carpets on Quarry Hill and flags afloat. You'd better tell the village."

"They seem to know," said Harry. "And Mother only told the chip shop."

"That'd be ample," said Mr Teesdale. "Coming with her husband I suppose?"

"No – with her daughter, it turns out," said James Bateman appearing at the back door, too, also hot and in wellingtons and with black hands from fighting sheep with a bottle of cough mixture. He wasn't back at college yet and would be helping Teesdales till October. He washed himself exactly like Mr Teesdale and then put his finger round the gingerbread bowl and got a wallop like his brother. The wallop was part of the recipe.

"She's coming," said James, "just really for a talk with Father. Not an interview. He says – it's 'planning'. She's on her way south from Scotland so she's looking in and staying two nights."

"Daughter has she?" said Mr Teesdale. "Don't look

97

more'n a bairn herself."

"Who's this?" said Mrs Teesdale coming in from chickens.

"A household word's coming to Light Trees," said Mr Teesdale – and explained.

"Oh – that one," said Mrs Teesdale. "Is she a friend then, Harry?"

"Not exactly. My father's met her once or twice."

"Then I'll speak as I find. I've never taken to her. She looks fast."

"You've got to be fast in that trade," said James. "In television it's the quick and the dead."

"She's going to find us fairly dead then," said Mrs Teesdale with a firm mouth.

But the following Friday afternoon when the household word's car stopped outside the Teesdale farm on the village street it did not appear to be so.

She sat with the face everybody knew so well lifted to the sun, and turned the head which everybody watched so often and knew even to the kink in the parting, and said in the voice which was part of the lives of everybody who just happened to be about at that time in the afternoon – though usually they were all round the back snoozing –

"Oh how divine!"

"How d'ye do?" said an old man who lived in a shed all day by the roadside, but today was sitting in front of it in a clean shirt.

"What a *beautiful* village! What *beautiful lupins*."

"Mrs Teesdale's," said the shed-sitter, graciously indicating her as she weeded about.

"Afternoon," said Mrs Teesdale.

"I'm looking for a house called Eight Trees."

"Light Trees, Light Trees," said Kendal, who wasn't busy with chimneys or the shop that day but happened to be out for an examination of the dry beck to see if any trout had lost their bearings and needed assistance. "Now that is very interesting. One of the explanations of the name is that it is a mistake by map makers. Eight Trees it should be, it's thought by many, but being uncertain of the lettering as many has been before and since, up to and including Shakespeare, two strokes got left off. *Light* Trees it is – and they called the next and last fell house Dark Trees for company though most folks round here calls it Ladford. You're on the track. Straight ahead."

"*Fas*cinating."

"Straight ahead," said old Mr Hewitson, "and round about. Upsides and over." He came up to the car and put his gnome head in at the passenger side.

The household word looked bewildered. "Straight ahead *and* round about?" You could hear the hard bit in the voice she used to get clear answers out of famous people who wanted to be mysterious.

"Take no heed of him," said Kendal. "Just straight ahead and keep going on up. When you're at the top there's Light Trees to the left of you."

"*Wonderful*," breathed the household word dropping her eye lashes, and a small fierce head beside her bowed over a book suddenly jutted upwards and said, "Oh let's get *on* Ma, for goodness sake. You know the way. We saw it on the map. You're just showing off." And the car whizzed under the Quarry Bridge and left the village gaping.

"What a little vixen!"

"I'd up-end her!"

"Poor young woman with a child of that description."

"Poor young child," said Grandad Hewitson, "with a dandy-dee of that sort for its mother."

When the car reached Light Trees the household word and her daughter were both rather set in the face, but soon the household word – when Harry's father had embraced her and guided the car into the fleece shed, where there was just room for it and taken her indoors – seemed happy again.

The fleeces in the shed were amusing, she said. And oh, wasn't Light Trees amusing? So dumpy and long and facing all the wrong way from the view. The view was amusing.

"Farmers never like a view," said Harry's mother. "They have too much of it all day. At night they want to get indoors and away from it."

"But don't their wives want a view? I suppose the poor little things never get asked what they want."

"The wives wouldn't wait to be asked," said Mrs. Bateman. "The wives rule the farm house. It's 'No boots in here', 'Wash yourself after that yard', and 'Don't let the dogs in or you stop out with them' since the beginning of time. No they don't want a view in the evening, they are too tired to look at it. The main thing is that there is only one door to these farm houses and that faces away from the east wind. They're the same as Viking houses you know. This one is hundreds of years old."

"*Darling* – you sound just like the quaint folk I've been talking to in the village street. Oh yes I'd *love* some tea, sweetie. What a heavenly rustic lounge! No don't bother about Poppet. She wants to stay in the car."

"In the car? In the fleece shed? She'll roast. She can't –"

"She's fine, lovey, she's fine. She's deep in a book. She'll come round in time."

"Oh dear – won't she want some tea?"

"A funny old man in the village dropped some gingerbread on her knee. I don't suppose for a minute it was clean, but we can't help it. Just leave her, darling – do come back. She's one of these clever, difficult ones. She's eleven. And we all know what *that* means."

"What does it mean?" Harry asked Bell later, telling about it over the sheep dips.

"Don't know," said Bell. "When I was eleven they'd have killed me if I'd sat in a car in a fleece shed when I'd been asked away on my holidays."

"Shall we go and get her out?"

They looked through the fleece shed window. The car had all its windows shut and appeared to be empty, but when they went inside there was a bent, small creature beside the driver's seat trying to read in semi-darkness. Bell knocked at the window.

The creature wound down the window and said "Go away" and wound it up again. Bell opened the door.

"Get out. Get out," said a violent, furious face covered in gingerbread crumbs.

"You're all over cake," said Bell.

The creature kicked him.

"OK – stay," said Bell.

"I'm reading."

"I'd have thought you were a bit old for Enid Blytons. Your Ma says you're doing your A levels or something."

The creature, like a hurtling cat, flung itself on Bell and Harry and all three somehow landed in the roly poly fleeces. Ten or twenty of them came bouncing down on top of them. Harry began to laugh and when he had spluttered out of the heap, laughed more.

"Shut up you *kid*," said the household word's daughter.

"You both look so daft – your great eyes flashing in all that wool," said Harry.

"Gis 'and," said Bell. Then the two of them pulled out the girl, whose glasses were broken, and who was still looking very dangerous. Bell grabbed her in the small of the back and held her by her tee shirt as the voices of people being polite to each other – talking more loudly than they need and laughing as if they were listening to themselves laughing – approached.

"We're all going for a walk," Harry's father called. "Going to Dark Trees. You children staying here?"

"No, coming," said Bell with a jaw of iron and frog-marched the girl forward.

"*I* don't want to come," said Harry with eyes astounded at Bell.

"We're all going," said Bell.

"Come my Poppet," called the household word and Poppet shook herself free and went and walked beside her mother, speaking to none.

"*Why're* we going? I don't want to go," said Harry. "Not with them."

"She ought to."

"Well that's her mother's affair."

"Sitting there sulking in fleeces."

"You're not her mother. What's it to you, Bell?"

"She's a rotten kid."

"So why're *we* going?"

"We've got to. Since we've made her."

"Oh I see. So you wouldn't have gone, wouldn't you, if she'd not played up? You're setting an example."

"I am not."

"You are. You're a prig, Bell Teesdale. Hey!"

"Stop it you two," called Harry's father.

The party, rather straggly, followed the road from Light Trees to the beck that sometimes runs on top of the ground and sometimes below it, then on up the hill, turning before the fell gate. Before dropping down Dark Trees' deep lane between its high stone walls, the household word and Poppet were shown the view. Hills like grey elephants ambled towards them from the south west. Hard blue and green peaks thrust down from the north. Direct west ahead, on the far horizon, swung the Saddleback with its patch of snow.

The household word who had been talking about Frozen Assets and the Unions said, "Oh yes. The Lake District," and went on talking.

Down at Dark Trees as they approached the yard gate and Tatton's half dozen uncontrolled dogs dancing, she was still talking. Chickens pecked about, a cow was happily rubbing its neck along the top of the byre door and snuffling, and Hannah was sitting on the porch quietly making a rag rug for the signal box. The household word was saying that England no longer existed and in her job she had learned to trust nobody in this awful country any more.

"Come in and see my cats," said Hannah to Poppet, holding out her hand. But Poppet turned her back, hanging over the brown beck that ran deep and busy alongside the farm door.

"D'you like our beck?" said Tatton. "That little bridge is old as history. Everyone comes taking photographs of it. D'you know our beck's never dried up they say in five hundred year? Not like all the rest. There's some becks around here you don't know where you are with. Here today and gone tomorrow like the gypsies. There's some becks, they tell me, that even is *called* gypsies – and they was called gypsies before there *was* any gypsies, if you can understand that. I'm not sure I can but it's in the dictionaries."

The household word had had to stop talking about how awful England was because everyone else was making such a racket about such things as what was to become of Hannah's chickens and where Tatton would be selling the dogs and who would look after the six new cherry trees planted last autumn for a windbreak. "Seems hard on them," said Hannah, "to come through '78 like us and we take off and they has to stay and die."

"Surely the next farmer will see to them?" said the household word in the voice she used on people who aren't being perfectly sensible.

"There's likely to be no next farmer," said Tatton. "The farm's rented. The rent's high. The sheep are heafed. That means you can't move them. They've been here since the Vikings this flock and they'd get nervous breakdowns if you tried to move them. The sheep and the land will maybe be rented separate, maybe by Teesdales, and the barns and byres, like Light Trees. But nobody but crackpots 'd want this house. It's the farthest on the fell. They'd have to be even more crackpots than Batemans. There's limits. No, Light Trees is a solitary house enough but if you don't live in Dark Trees through the winter it'll fall to pieces. Dark Trees'll be a ruin five years from now."

"But such a *beautiful* house!" And the household word, a light of a very disturbing sort appearing in her eye, swept past Hannah – though she had not yet been invited in – over the doorstep of Dark Trees and started briskly opening and shutting doors. When she saw the great grandfather clock and the meal chest and the settle and the man's knitting chair the size of a throne, she said, "Did you say you were going to live in a *signal box*?"

"Oh these we're leaving – or selling for a pound or two. They'd not be wanted most places. They were born here in the house and lived here all their lives."

"I expect you've had the dealers after them?"

"Oh, we couldn't do with dealers. We'll maybe put an advert in *The Herald* for someone to take them away."

The household word asked if she could see the bedrooms and look at the plumbing. When she came down – an uneasy, glum sort of feeling had settled over everybody – she asked how much money the owner wanted for the house. When she was told her eyes became brighter and clearer than ever.

Going out again to find Poppet who was sitting on the gate with her back to everybody, the household word looked carefully at the thick strong walls, the tiny, deep-set windows, the huge old door that had been made and opened and shut for the first time by somebody who wore sheep-skins and rags on his feet and spoke a language nobody in the yard today would understand and who only ever went to the village on special occasions – to sell sheep or see the great Lord of the Marches set off to the coronation in his rubies and pearls. The household word said, "You say the water-supply is good? That's what is usually the matter with these places I suppose, lack of water?"

Tatton, who thought very slowly, could not tell why his heart was heavy when he said again – as of course he had to – that no, the beck had never dried up in five hundred years.

"*Simply* wonderful," said the household word on the way home. "So *cheap*! I'm most definitely tempted. Poppet darling – we're *definitely* tempted, aren't we?"

The London father said, "But my dear girl – what about your work? You would never get up here. The place would stand empty for months of the year."

"Not at all. I'd let it to friends. There are dozens of people in the media just *longing* for a place like this to relax in. And a wonderful place for parties!"

"They'd not like the weather. It's not always like today. Is it, Teesdale?"

Mr Teesdale was coming past them down the fell with long strides behind a little cluster of sheep. Two dogs swept round, holding the sheep together.

"What a wonderful country scene," said the household word. "How marvellous to see a real *shepherd*." Mr Teesdale gave her a quick sharp look.

"Weather's not as I'd like it even today," said he. "Too bright. We'll not get dipped tomorrow."

"But it's *glorious* weather."

"Let's wait on," said Mr Teesdale.

At the beck that was seldom at home above ground they let him pass them with the sheep and paused on the tiny culvert bridge. The beck bottom was thick with green grass, fat thistles and purple and yellow wild pansies. Lady's smock was like clouds of white midges. There were harebells. It was a garden.

But – "Hey! Look!" said Harry.

Coming towards them over the green grass moved something blue. You could see the edge to it, getting nearer. It was water, soaking steadily along down the green channel reflecting the sky. When it reached them it curled quietly about some stones under the culvert and passed beneath them and out the other side, so that where a moment before had been a green garden was now a blue waterway.

"Did you ever see such a thing!" said the London people.

"Only but once or twice," said Bell. "It means there's something up below."

"Up *below*," said the household word, "oh I say!"

"Deep under the ground," said Bell.

The sky darkened during supper and during Monopoly the rain began. When Mr Teesdale came up to fetch Bell and Harry – for Harry had given up his bed to Poppet and was sleeping at Bell's during the visit – the rain was streaming, rattling down and the wind was rising fast. It was very warm. During the evening there had been several, solitary, great claps of thunder.

"Look sharp you two," said Teesdale, "let's get down yon Quarry Hill. Get your coats on. This puts finish to any dipping in the morning."

"Is it certain that the weather will be like this tomorrow?" said the household word in the tone she used.

Mr Teesdale gave her the look he used and said "Certain."

From his bed at Bell's – a Z bed with a feather mattress bulging all over it like clouds – Harry said, "Bell, whatever shall we do?"

Grunt said Bell.

"To stop her? We've got to stop her. We can't let her come. It would be terrible. All the awful people she'd bring. London people shrieking about."

"You're London people. You don't shriek about."

"Her lot would. And that Poppet!"

"Aye – that Poppet."

"That Poppet'd bring her awful friends, too."

"She'll not have many friends I'd think. Not by the way she plays Monopoly. Win, win, win. Grab, grab, grab."

"Just think of her always here! Every single holiday. Just think of her at Tatton and Hannah's. Flaunting about."

"She doesn't flaunt exactly. Her Ma flaunts. That Poppet grumps."

"One flaunting, one grumping, all the friends shrieking. I'd not come. I'd not come here any more. I'd stay home. It's not *fair*."

"Oh, give over," said Bell. "Get to sleep. Sommat'll fetch up."

"Hey, we could do summat. To Tatton's beck. Dry it up. It's right small where it springs up in Dukerdale."

Snore said Bell.

"We've seen it. We could dam it. We could *divert* it. Hey, Bell, tomorrow when you've no work since we're not dipping we could go on up and *divert* it."

Bell stopped snoring and said against the roaring torrents attacking the window, and the wailing wind, "Grand time for damming becks – day like tomorrow's going to be."

"But what shall we do, then Bell. Oh what shall we do?"

"See what tomorrow brings. It oftimes brings summat."

"Not a dry beck though."

And most certainly it did not. That day was the wettest day in Westmorland since they began to keep records. Four inches of rain fell in a night and at dawn it was still coming down as hard. The Light Trees' beck that had come up pretty and blue for an airing went quite out of its mind. It pounced and foamed and crashed about in a positive brainstorm. It covered its own green channel and turned into a brown-white spate. It slopped and foamed over half the valley and swept in to the Home Field. The culvert completely disappeared. It cut off Dark Trees, of course, starting with their telephone so that no one could find out how Tatton and Hannah were managing. Everyone at Light Trees just sat. Or looked out of steamy windows. The household word smoked cigarettes. Poppet went up to her room and locked the door. After lunch which was difficult because the kitchen got so hot that the heat and stife came rolling across in to the living room, every one began a tremendous yawning. Mr Bateman longed to go off and do some work but felt he couldn't with a visitor. Mrs Bateman found she hadn't a single thing to talk to the household word about. The household word sat frowning at her beautiful rose red finger nails.

Then there was an unholy noise in the yard.

It was Hannah.

Somehow she had crossed the culvert and she stood weeping – sopped to the skin on Light Trees' porch step she wept, with moss in her hair.

"We're flooded," she cried, "flooded out. Worse'n ever in our lives. We've the dogs and the chickens in the bedrooms and Tatton's trying to get the cow up too but it's stuck on the stairs. The knitting chair's afloat and the grandfather clock's going to have a ring round its knees till the end of its days. If it goes on we'll all be ont' roof and Tatton says he can't get a cow on a roof. Bedrooms yes, he says, roof no. And the yard is like Amazonian torrents.

"The television's safe," she said with a polite nod to the household word. "It's up on a wardrobe and Tatton put his back out lifting it, which is probably why he's in fixtures with the cow.

"The telephone," she added, "got drowned."

The household word said she thought she might be more use staying behind to look after Light Trees, but otherwise everyone – even Poppet who had been up in her bedroom staring, Mrs Bateman said, in a real sulk at the lustre tea pot – set off to Dark Trees to help. The rain was lighter. You could wade now just to your thighs where the culvert must be, and up the hill and down the lane was not too bad – but no view of distant mountains today. When they reached Dark Trees quite a lot of people were there already from the other side of Dukerdale over the high limestone pavements on the rigg. Tatton was hanging out of his bedroom window looking very doleful and saying he was really a railway man, and everything was just as Hannah had said.

A ladder was found in a barn and waved in Tatton's direction and encouraging sounds were made like "Jump man, and swim," – but Tatton wouldn't on account of the dogs and the cow. There was a great deal of splashing and shouting and advice-giving for perhaps an hour when some-one – it was Poppet who was standing with Eileen – noticed that the water level was dropping. Or perhaps.

Half an hour later it was certain. It was decidedly dropping. And half an hour after that Mr Teesdale got in through the front door and said hello to the lid of the meal chest and gathered up the new rag rug as it floated by. Another half hour and you could actually see the feet of the knitting chair looking very rheumaticky and the rounded edges of the fine stone flags on the floor. Tatton and the cow came down the stairs and the cow rushed wildly out in to the yard. After being in a bedroom it never felt quite the same again – and neither did the bedroom.

By nightfall you could stand on Light Trees' culvert bridge again and watch the water just filling the arch below, boiling and gurgling still, and brown and not blue, but nicely behaved now, not frightening. Wrapped round in rugs, Hannah and Tatton came to Light Trees for the night – in fact for quite a lot of nights for their house was not habitable for a long time. They were very happy with the Batemans' living room floor and hot soup, then dinner and warm blankets. But they were extremely talkative and didn't seem to want to sleep at all. The household word – who had examined her finger nails very thoroughly by now – said that she on the other hand felt like an early night.

She and Poppet left next morning – which was fine and sparkling like the first day of God – and did not mention coming back. "A *thrilling* visit," said the household word. "Wonderful place, darlings – *so* exciting!" Great kissings all round went on and then she got in the car where Poppet had already seated herself, glaring fiercely at her knees. "Goodbye Poppet," said Mrs Bateman, but she did not reply.

"So that's the end of that," said everyone. Mrs Bateman got the red and white quilts out of hiding and put them on the beds again. "Thanks be," said Harry. "The finish of them."

But it was not. A week or so later came a post card from Poppet with glamorous palm trees and a white beach on it and it said "Thank you for a lovely, lovely, lovely time. Oh I do wish I could come back! Mother says not now. Oh, it was all wonderful. Lots and lots and lots of love from Poppet."

"I don't think I understand girls," said Mrs Bateman, "only having had boys."

"Well, neither do I," said Mrs Teesdale, "and I've got one."

"Neither do I," said Harry.

"I do," said Bell. "They're cracked."

Eileen understood Poppet though, and so did old Mr Hewitson, for next year he went to the station to meet her when she came to stay with Eileen.

Eileen had married a farmer and gone to live at Dark Trees and Poppet stayed with them for many holidays for many years. She fed the chickens and gathered the eggs and mixed the gingerbreads and grew a very chattery, cheerful girl.

And the beck beside the farm house door ran smoothly along.

8 · Table Talk

It was Appleby Horse Fair and all the roads near and far were threaded with gypsies. They came from all over England, and had done every year since the gypsies started. There had been other people ahead of them – starting they say with the Greeks on their way to Scotland to leave stories and bagpipe dances behind them. Then the brooding Celts with their copper pans and choppers. Then the Romans who travelled light but left re-arrangements behind them. Then King Arthur and his knights who fell asleep in a room under Richmond Castle and are still there if we could only find the way down. Then the dreadful Eric Bloodaxe arrived who bit the Stainmore dust, and the unspeakable Scotsman, Malcolm the Red, who burned Appleby to the ground twice, before the Danes came and looked about more sanely and thought that this would be a nice place to settle down.

But even after all this, it was still a long time ago that the blue-eyed gypsies arrived for the Horse Fair, appearing by stages and to be seen in all the lay-bys of the road from the south which the Romans called Watling Street, like the swallows back from Africa. And like the swallows they never stopped to tell you why.

Their visits made – and still make – difficulties. Gypsies make people who are born of go-ahead Danish or Celtic stock uneasy. Vikings like neatness and hard work and no mess. Celts are less fussy, but they believe in talking, not sliding off and out of sight. And gypsy fortune-tellings drive people of the Hollow Land mad because Viking or Celt or whatever they are, they know their fortune is in the weather and they know the weather better than any gypsy for they have to be out in it working night and day. The arrival of the gypsies occasions a lot of drawing in of lips as their battered cars and shiny caravans come sliding back down the lanes.

One year, at the same time as the Appleby Horse Fair, there was an important sheep sale at Hawes – a bad arrangement. Every one needed to go to one or the other or both – the Teesdales in particular because they specialised in little black-faced Swaledale sheep which needed to be seen, as Swaledales were beginning to be less popular. "We have to go – it's our shop window," said Bell. "Our sheep-window," said Grandpa Hewitson.

The Batemans had been to the first day of the Horse Fair and were missing the sale as it was nearly time for London again and Mrs Bateman was wanting to go with Mrs Teesdale to a wonderful new antique shop that had set up over Stainmore. She had left it late as usual – this was her last day.

"The whole village'll be empty this afternoon," said Mrs Teesdale. "It's a pity with gypsies about. But I've got to go. I've got to keep Mrs Bateman right about prices."

"Well then go," said Mr Teesdale. "There's old Jimmie Meccer in his shed. He'll watch all's well in the village."

"Crack lot of good he'd be. He's hardly the use of his feet.

No more has that fond dog. I've never heard it yap. Nor old Jimmie yap. Not more'n three words. Sitting there in that shed-back with his face like a bladder of lard morning till moonrise."

"Well, make him sit in front of it then. It's fine weather. He can have a stick over his knees along of his walking aid."

"I'd sooner he sat at the telephone box down the street. We could sit him there with a fivepenny bit if owt came up urgent."

So Jimmie Meccer, armed with a fivepenny piece and his dog, was set up in the telephone box with the door propped open. He filled the doorway so thoroughly that it was uncertain whether he would be able to reach round to the receiver if any trouble did come.

"We could sit him in backwards," said someone.

"Well then he'd not be able to keep watch."

"There's a mirror."

"It's above his head. Anyway he'd not look much threat sat with his back to everything."

They lumped him about for a while, this way and that way, and finally had him looking fairly obvious and considerable. They made him practise stretching backwards to the receiver, which wasn't a complete success.

"He'd look more to be reckoned with in a hat," said someone. "Batemans of Light Trees has hats. James brings them home from foreign holidays. We'll borrow a Light Trees' hat."

So Jimmie Meccer, in a straw sombrero, a stick across his knees, a dog at his feet and the walking aid close by but not noticeable in the bushes, sat magnificently in the telephone box to guard the village.

"Mind we could give him a gun," said Kendal, sensational as usual.

"Heaven forbid!"

"I'm no fool," said Jimmie suddenly. "There seems some

idea going about that I'm a fool. I'll not watch your blessed
houses if you don't think on. It's not owt to me what any
gypsies take. There's nothing of mine they'd want. For all
I'll ever lose I could sit here and watch them crawling in and
out of all your houses with your three piece suites and silver
sheep-cups. I'm not likely to bestir myself if I'm not appreci-
ated."

"Come on now, Jimmie," they said more kindly, "we'll
bring you presents back. You'll be grand."

Mrs Teesdale and Mrs Bateman set out for the antique shop
about half past two. It was only a few miles over Stainmore,
over the wonderful old road the Greeks and Celts and
Romans and Vikings, Angles, Saxons and the odd Jute had
used before them more adventurously. Ghost upon ghost
haunts this road from Greta Bridge where a spirit got caught
under a stone and twice they've had to put her back; to the
blue ghost you can see sometimes on bright sunny afternoons
near Bowes, the wife of a Saxon lord still wearing her Saxon
dress, but without her head; to the white ghost near the old
mines who walks quietly in her apron. These are only a few
of the people you are likely to see. Another – very much alive
– is Mrs Teesdale's cousin at the wool shop at Brough. Mrs
Teesdale hadn't seen her for at least three weeks and as they
were passing the door they felt they must just look in.

Time passed. "Dear me," said Mrs Teesdale at 4.30, "this
antique shop on Stainmer'll be shut if we don't mind."

"Well, but stop for your tea," said the cousin.

"No – we've left the whole village in charge of Jimmie
Meccer this afternoon and there's gypsies about, and he'll be
asleep as like as not."

The cousin said she'd take it badly if they didn't stop for
their teas. Armed guards against gypsies, she said, were just
ridiculous. In her opinion gypsies were not so bad at all.
There were ordinary thieves about now, yes. Believe it or

not, yes. Her father had never once had to take his front door key off the kitchen beam where he'd found it when he moved in to his farm fifty years back, but now she'd heard, because of the motorways, they were putting up grid things even in the post office and how they were to get the eggs and that over the counter she did not know. This old road was a godsend to thieves. When the trains were running down the bottom in the old days and before motor cars, her grandfather said there wasn't a thing on the road – green grass growing on it. Now there's fleets of motor coaches and caravans and boats on top of cars and bikes standing on their heads on sports-car lids and you can get a real good prawn cocktail, she'd heard, at the Old Spital Inn where they used to keep the Hand of Glory.

At length – long length – they got away, with a great deal of waving and calling and wool for winter jerseys. Hold fast, said Mrs Teesdale as she reined in the car and then let it leap furiously the eighteen inch step at the turn off on to Stainmore – engineering that would have made the Romans wince and fall on their swords. They sped across the moor among the dotted farms and up on to the top of the fells again to the Castle Antique Shop.

As they swept down its long drive they passed a car travelling fast in the other direction, then came upon the Castle moat and tremendous studded door – the sort of door that Eric Bloodaxe might have been carried through dead to be laid out by his lesser lords, all doffing their horned helmets, upon some great table top.

There, in fact, inside the antique shop's great door was just such a table top. A magnificent, ancestral king of tables stood there, the size of a caravan or a small chapel. "Put curtains round it," said Mrs Teesdale, "and you could call it a four-poster."

The antique dealer was standing by this table, stroking it as they came in and waved them quite dreamily past him.

"Go where you like," he said. "All the ground floor's on view. Everything for sale. Go as you please."

"What a huge old table," said Mrs Bateman.

"Just arrived," said the antique dealer, stroking away. "I've never seen anything like it."

"Hmmm," said Mrs Teesdale.

"Don't ask to buy it. It's on its way to London. It's very early. *Very* early. Pre-Reformation," said the dealer.

"Goodness," said Mrs Teesdale. "It's just like mine was. We chopped it up when we got the units." The dealer closed his eyes.

Mrs Bateman went up to the table. There was a huge old drawer in its side.

She pulled it out crooked, with a knocking noise. It was smoothly made within. The boards that made its top were ridged and silky from hundreds of years of scouring. The dark wood had turned silvery, like driftwood on a clean shore.

"Before King Henry the Eighth," said the dealer. "Oh, well before. I've not seen another so fine. It's just arrived. I bought if from the gypsies. They left as you arrived. Used to deal in horses and pots and pans, the gypsies. But mending pans has gone, and horses are scarce. Antiques are easier and gypsies – my, they know their stuff! They have the chance to learn, too – they get a view through the back door of every farm they want to call at. They can see with one flick of an eye-lash while they wait for a can of milk to be filled or a dozen eggs, every stick of furniture in a back kitchen. They know the value, too. They're clever. They're cleverer than us folk are gypsies."

"Is it valuable?" asked Mrs Bateman, stroking in her turn the old ridges and whorls and knots on the table top, worn bare as the fells and in contours not unlike them.

"Between twelve and thirteen hundred pounds," said the dealer.

Mrs Teesdale who had been prowling around by herself in the back of the shop and picking things up and putting them down again, saying in rather loud asides "*Over* priced, *over* priced," came up and looked long and hard at the table. The two women gazed at one another.

"Yes. Twelve to thirteen hundred pounds," said the dealer. "When these gypsies arrived here half an hour ago with this table on the top of their car – pressing it so hard in to the ground I thought they'd step out with flat heads – they said, 'We've a table.'

"'Where from?' says I.

"'A back kitchen. Been standing there for ever. Folk didn't want it. Did them a favour. Took it off them. Grand old table.'

"I played it very quiet, ladies."

"Back *kitchen* table?" said Mrs Teesdale thoughtfully. She drew her hands that had kneaded dough about on tables for a good many years – not to mention girdle cakes, tea-cakes, sally luns, maids of honour, scones, biscuits, pastry and granny loaf, milk fadge, fatty cakes and swedish fingers. She said, "Well now!"

"So I thought," said the dealer, "my stars! I'm in for a fortune – maybe thirteen hundred and fifty pounds. 'Nice table,' says I, 'nobody wants this sort of thing nowadays though. Not with kitchen units and such-like. I'll find it hard to get rid of again but I'll give you a fiver.'

"'That you will not,' said the gypsy standing on the spot you're on now with his eyes all slant. The other feller was sat picking his teeth in the porch.

" 'Well,' said I. 'Make it ten.'

" 'Make it between twelve hundred and thirteen hundred,' said he. 'You'll get near fourteen hundred in the south.'

"So what about that? They're no fools aren't gypsies. We settled for a thousand and they made off fairly satisfied – not over thrilled though. Level headed. Off down the road to

London. I got their car number mind – I've my reputation to consider."

"It's a nice story," said Mrs Bateman.

"Hmmm," said Mrs Teesdale yet again. "*Back* kitchen."

There was not a word out of her as they went whirling over the hill to Brough Sowerby, twisting into Kaber, through the ruined railway bridge to Barras. The south of Stainmore rolled out before them with not a sign of all the history that had happened all over it. The car flew along. You felt that if the Saxon lady on her horse had suddenly appeared in her blue dress and without her head, Mrs Teesdale would hardly have swerved.

"Aren't we going rather fast?" asked Mrs Bateman. "I suppose we are a bit late. It was a lovely shop. My word, what a wonderful table." She held tight to the needlework picture she had bought and closed her eyes and prayed as they nearly hit a passing sheep.

"Hmmm."

"Didn't you think so?"

"Wonderful no," said Mrs Teesdale, "wonderful no."

They arrived back in the village where people were beginning to arrive home from the long day at the fair. Bell and Harry and Mr Bateman and Mr Teesdale and Old Hewitson were unloading and exclaiming over sheep and prizes from the back of the trailer. "Fust prize for best-beast-overall," cried Harry in a voice his friends in London never heard.

"That's right then," said Mrs Teesdale striding past without a glance.

Up the village street she strode to where Jimmie Meccer sat outside his telephone box like the Buddha in the evening sun, eating a slice of prize apple pie. "Well now, Jimmie," she said, "how did you get on?"

"A right quiet day," said Jimmie.

"And no intruders?"

"Nowt of owt," said Jimmie, "nowt of any kind."

"No gypsies?"

"No. Mebbe a car or two went by through to Quarry Hill and passed down back again when they found Dark Trees' dead-end at the fell gate."

"You had your little nap I dare say?"

"Not at all. Mind I had my thoughts like usual."

"Deep thoughts," said Mrs Teesdale and marched across the road into Jimmie's house and out the back and in to his shed where there were two great bags of potatoes, bridles of long-dead horses, and Jimmie's stack of winter kindling. And a space. A large space. On the floor in the middle of it stood Jimmie's supper – a big lemon jelly setting nicely. Jimmie had been putting jellies to set on his back shed table for years and years and years.

"My table! My table's gone! Well bye! Well bye! It's been spirited off. My rickety rackety old table."

They caught them just north of Luton, thanks to Mrs Teesdale's wits, and the dealer having taken their number.

At first the police said that they would have to look after the thousand pounds and the table as evidence until the trial came up; but when they saw the size of the table they weren't sure it would fit in the police station and decided they could give the thousand pounds back to the dealer, and the table back to Jimmie.

But Jimmie said no.

If it was all the same, he said, he would like the thousand pounds and the dealer could sell the table again. He was quite definite about this and everyone was astonished – Jimmie not being renowned for being definite. Or really for being anything except good at sitting about.

"The thousand pounds," said Jimmie. And in the end he got it.

Then he did get rather topsy-turvy – the doctor said it was delayed shock – and had to be taken into hospital for a few days, and the village said, "He's finished!"

But this wasn't true either, for in the hospital the doctors got a good look at him and told him that there were things to be done for legs nowadays and with a couple of plastic hips they could have him skipping down the village street like a new lamb.

And all this happened.

Jimmie paraded that autumn down the village like the Lord of the Marches and his dog watched him, utterly terrified.

Later Jimmie announced that he was off to South America to see his sister who was very comfortable there, her father having inherited a fortune from the Meccer who'd gone storming off up the fell one dinner time, leaving his marmalade duff untouched, to make a fortune.

And like that Meccer, Jimmie Meccer married somebody in South America and never came back.

And it was months and months and months before people had stopped examining their old bits and pieces in their back sheds. But there was never another table found like the one that was kidnapped by the gypsies – if, of course, it was the gypsies, for the address of the thieves turned out to be Park Lane, London. No, there was never another discovery like the one on the day of the Appleby Horse Fair.

9 · Tomorrow's Arrangements

Some things, if you know enough, can be worked out in advance. For example, a total eclipse of the sun. Other things are considered accidents.

The visit of Henry Roberto Hewitson III from South America to North Westmorland was considered an accident. For who on earth could have known that because Mrs Bateman left it so late in her holiday to visit the antique shop on North Stainmore, that Jimmie Meccer would go to South America? And in South America that he would meet someone who could threaten all that he had left behind?

When Jimmie reached South America his sister invited to meet him every local Hewitson, Metcalf and Teesdale who had left the Pennine fells and mines in the hard times long ago, and their children and grandchildren. One of these grandchildren was Henry Hewitson III – a man with a very rigid mind and a tremendous lot of money. As a result of the meeting there occurred in this rigid mind a little chink, like a chink in Pennine limestone made by the minerals in the hard water flowing over it; the little chink that in years to come turns hard hills into honeycomb and makes out of solid-looking rock great tunnels and caves and pot-holes and deep unknown cathedrals, running sometimes with water which falls roaring over underground precipices, whirlpooling and surging along, so that above, as you tread over smooth green turf, small yellow pansies and little blood red toadstools, you hear a sort of beating under your feet, like a heart beating strongly.

Henry Roberto Hewitson III's heart, however, nobody could imagine beating strongly. It was difficult to imagine it beating at all. More likely, under his silky silvery suit and his silky silvery tie and his shirt so white it made you blink, inside his rib-cage, much more likely you would have found a neat little silvery box clicking away with bleeping signals to keep Henry Hewitson III moving. Henry's blood was hard to imagine too. Cut him and out would come – surely – not blood but a clear and silvery powerful fluid rather like expensive gin.

Henry Hewitson III was a specialist in money, and in mining, and he got up in the morning and went to bed at night without a fear in his head that anything might ever go against him. He was more successful, and grander in every way than the other people at Jimmie's party and he stood a little to one side of them. He only stayed for half an hour as he had his private aeroplane to catch. He stood in his silvery suit with his slim and silvery brief-case in his hand and spoke to nobody much. When he went to say goodbye to Jimmie Meccer, Jimmie took his clean pale hand and said,"Now then – *Henry* Hewitson? You'll be Mary's auntie's mother's grandson then? Old Jimmie Hewitson's wife up at Light Trees. Light Trees was always Hewitsons. You'll have to pay it a visit."

And in the aeroplane going home, Henry's small junction-box of a heart clicked away and his pale eyes stared straight ahead of him at the back of the seat in front because he never was one to look out of windows: and then crack! The little chink that set the landscape melting and changing underfoot happened in his mind.

"Bright Trees?" "Eight Trees?" What had Jimmie Metcalf said? Hadn't there been something? Something his father had told him? No – his grandfather. Long ago, when he was hardly at school. "Light Trees will be Henry's. It's always gone to a Hewitson through the cousins. Fine old house away up in the fells. Wonderful land, stuffed full of minerals never worked out. Left lying there under the ground when the slump came. Maybe oil there, I always thought."

But then the aeroplane began to land. The chink sealed over leaving the surface of Henry's mind as smooth as silk for many years.

Down in Teesdales' farm kitchen many years later, Mrs Teesdale took a letter from the postman with a South American stamp on it. "Jimmie Meccer," she said. "He still keeps writing. He's early for Christmas this time. It'll have to keep till tonight. It's hay-time."

She stood the letter on the kitchen mantelpiece and got on with packing baskets with field dinners they were carrying up on a harness to the men. It was a doubtful day but Mr Teesdale and Bell and Eileen's husband had decided to start. They were beginning by tradition with the Home Field, which always had to be done before Batemans arrived for their holidays. Nobody remembered now, after so many, many summers, why the Home Field had to be cut before Batemans arrived. And in so many, many summers nobody remembered one so queer as this. First burning sun, then long soaking days of rain, then thunder, then sun again for six weeks. Never two days right together. Poppet Teesdale said she'd never heard them say anything good about any year, but Grandpa Hewitson said no. This one was different. Old Hewitson sat about a lot now and was far past even thistling – for it was the year 1999 – but his memory was perfect. "The last time we had a summer like this," he said, "was 1927, when there was an eclipse of the sun. As there's to be this year. Though whether I'll be turning out to see this one is something still to be thought about."

"You'll see it, Grandpa. We'll carry you on up."

"Carry me on up? Sounds as if you're angels."

"On up on to the top. You know what we mean. We'll all be going. On up above Light Trees for the eclipse."

"You'll not get me up there this time. I'm beyond going up the Nine Standards."

"Everyone'll be up the Nine Standards. Except the odd crank like old Kendal who's booked his place years ago for Cornwall, where it's to be total."

"Total eclipse," said Grandpa, "total eclipse of the sun. They held a total eclipse up here in 1927 on this very spot. Better than it'll be this time where we're a fraction off the track say. In '27 we all got let out of school for it. We had to lie on our backs in t'school yard with little bits of black glass in front of our eyes. We laid out in rows, all laughing on and chit-chattering. There was old Granny Crack's lass lying out next to me in her black woollen stockings and button shoes. Alice Crack she was then from over Kisdon. Bright red hair. By – she was a talker. She changed. 'Alice Crack,' she said – the school teacher – 'Alice Crack, if you don't stop talking, we'll all go inside and you won't any of you see it and if you don't see it now you'll never see it for there won't be another till 1999 and that one won't be total.' 'Don't see why I shouldn't see that'un,' says Alice Crack, 'I'll be scarcely ninety. You won't see it though, will you, Miss?' So she had to go inside and she didn't see it. She had to sit at her desk. She cried an'all."

"Well, she'll see it this time," said Mrs Teesdale. "We promised we'd take her. Lord knows how. Maybe in a pram. She's a fair weight yet, too."

"I don't ever see," said Poppet who was over for hay-time from down the road, her husband being up the fell all day with the rest – "why it's got to be up at the Nine Standards we have to do things."

"Always was," said her mother-in-law, "it's a tradition."

"Time some traditions was looked over and sorted out," said Old Hewitson. "Traipsing here and there. The Jubilee – all the Jubilees. King Charles's wedding. The old Queen Mother's funeral. Why some of them still goes up for Guy Fawkes to this day."

"Old Mr Kendal says that people have gone up there since before the Romans," said Poppet. "He says the Nine Standards are probably Roman soldiers turned to stone. Says it's part of the Lost Legion of the Ninth they used to write about in the old children's books. They never got to Scotland, Mr Kendal said. They only got as far as the Rigg and got turned to stone."

"Kendal," said Old Hewitson, "always read over-many fond books."

"He says before the Romans the Rigg is where the Celts used to drive their cattle through the smoke."

"That," said Grandpa Hewitson, "is pure ridiculous Kendal talk. No folks, not even Romans, was daft enough to take cattle up yonder."

"For sacrifice and that," said Poppet's girl, Anne.

"It'd be sacrifice all right, sacrificing good money int' market. They'd be good for nowt, hiked all the way up to them Nine Standards and put through smoke."

"Nor us neither going gowking at eclipses of the sun eleven o'clock in the morning of a good day's hay-making," said Bell, coming in to see after the baskets setting off. "I'm warning you I'm not going looking at eclipses on August whatever 'tis. I'm cracking on."

"You'll not get much done int' dark."

"It's not going to last five minutes."

"There's the coming and going of it. And it's bad luck not to take notice."

"It'll be darkness all right," said Old Hewitson.

"All darkness is darkness."

"No. Darkness is all sorts. And let me tell you, Bell, darkness from eclipses of the sun is not like owt else. It's neither darkness of night nor gloom of twilight nor darkness from the Helm Wind over Dufton, like there can be on a bright day."

"Darkness is darkness. I don't care about missing out on seeing some darkness."

"There's more'n darkness about it. Stars come out. You can spot the planets – Venus, Mercury. Birds stop singing. All animals up at Light Trees from Hartley Birket to Nateby Birket will be falling silent and standing mazed."

"Aye well. I dare say we'll not ignore it, Grandpa."

"And another thing I remember. Lying there int' school yard. Under them currant bushes she kept. You remember them currant bushes, Bell?"

"Not there in my time, Grandpa. Nor yet in Dad's."

"Well under these currant bushes and the two-three trees they had there was little wee bits o' light scattered. For an hour before, maybe. Little pieces like of light, and as the sky changed to like sunset, every little speckle under them trees turned crescent-shaped like the new moon."

"There'll not be yon up the Nine Standards. There's not a tree to speak of. And Standards themselves is too solid to show any crescent moons scattered about."

"Which is why I'll be staying down here," said Old Hewitson. "I'll seat myself int' garden by Mary's lupins. Alice Crack, the Egg Witch, can go gallivanting in prams."

"Anyways, it'll likely rain," said Bell, who had grown over

126

the years more like his father than his father had ever been. "Like it's about to do today. Come on. Let's get moving. It's nine o'clock already."

"In my day," said Old Hewitson, "hardest part of hay-time was over by nine o'clock of a morning. That's when we rested, nine o'clock, horses being tired out. Good fast go at it we had from five int' morning till eight. Then breakfast. In the hedge back. Tatie pies. You could only cut properly with dew upon the ground. People got out of their beds them days. I were called out at five from under my bedroom window. I were earning by time I were eleven."

"You's talking of scything days."

"I'se talking of horses. Same as it's horses again now. There was scything and leading with horses, then cutting and leading with horses. Then away went the horses and in came the machinery. And now, since the oil went, we're back to the horses. I never thought I'd live to see the old tractors go. Grand they were, though dangerous. Rolled on you many times more often than any horse if you didn't handle them right. I liked the old tractors mind. Historic."

"I don't know," said Eileen to her mother as they started to walk the Quarry Hill, empty these days of lorries and with creepers showering down the deserted limestone cliffs, "we get more History lessons the older he gets. His memory gets sharper every day." "It's better than with some," said her mother. She shifted the heavy harness which held the buckets for the field dinners. "He doesn't go in for holy traditions, saying things never should change and the only good things are the things that are over. He's all for the present and the future still. Grandpa's himself."

"Oh but he likes traditions."

"Aye but he casts about among them. Thinks them out. He's not like poor old Jimmie Meccer, still wambling on about being home-sick after all these years. There was a letter from him this morning?"

"Is he right?"

"I don't know. Hadn't the time to read it. It'll likely be usual sort of an affair. His letters don't change. He might be still in his shed."

But, "Oh my word!" said she later, in the warm, wet, impossible morning, with no hay-making done and back down at the farm again. "Oh my word – but this isn't from Jimmie Meccer. Lord knows who it's from except he calls hisself a Hewitson and he's from South America somewhere-other and he's coming here."

"Here?"

"Aye. To us. Any day. He's on his way."

"Who is he? How's he getting to travel?"

"Well I don't know. He'll be great auntie's lad's lad. Or lad's lad's lad. I'd think. Or someone. Wonderful letter-paper he uses. Beautiful script. He says he's booked at a hotel."

"Coming to see the old home likely. Is he bringing Jimmie back?"

"No. He says he's not seen Jimmie in donkey's years. Not since Jimmie's arrival party. Says he meant to come here, but with the oil crisis and his work – now he's retired. And he's coming about – he's coming about his *inheritance*!"

"Inheritance," said Mr Teesdale coming in thinking of more vital matters like getting in some investigations for fluke worm in mules since the rain had dished everything else. He carried the tools for fluke worm searches and a black frown. "Inheritance. He can inherit this weather. We've not much else to give him. He'll soon be away back again. Right out of his depths he'll be here."

"Inheritance," said Mrs Teesdale reading, "of the farm house Light Trees."

"Oh," said Bell.

"Ah," said Old Hewitson. "Ah. Aha. That."

128

And everyone was silent, like the birds at an eclipse of the sun.

On August the first, Henry Roberto Hewitson III arrived in a gleaming car and unannounced. He knocked on Teesdales' door and it was opened at once because Mrs Teesdale still did her own floors and was on her knees behind it washing the lino. She was in her sacking apron because she had been feeding hens earlier and doing the other dirty jobs while the fire got hot for the oven and she changed in to her cooking pinny. She looked first at the car and said "A car!" Then she looked at her cousin many times removed, his silvery suit, moustache and head of hair and no-coloured eyes, and he looked at her broad brown face and broad brown hands and eyes as blue as the headless woman's dress. She said, "Are you coming' in?"

"I am Henry Roberto Hewitson III."

"You're Auntie Win's brother-in-law's father's son's boy and you're the image of William!"

"William – ?"

"William my only other cousin who died. Of Whin Gill over Brough Sowerby way."

"I am from Brazil."

"My but I can see it in the hands! No hands for a farmer or a miner we always said. Didn't know where they'd hailed from them narrow hands. And them shoulders! Well! He died young, poor William. He never prospered."

Henry Roberto Hewitson III who had done nothing but prosper since the day he was born walked behind her to the kitchen with a blank expression.

He was introduced. Mr Teesdale and Bell were out but Eileen was over with Poppet. Eileen was often over with Poppet and Poppet's Anne. They were talking about cake entries for Appleby Horse Fair and how to get them there. Old Hewitson was there – close up against the fire though it was a hot day. He sat at the edge of a big stretch of newly-washed stone floor because all the rag rugs were out airing in the yard with the cats, and most of the furniture.

"You are moving house?" said Henry Hewitson III. "I apologise. I should have made an appointment."

"Moving house? No – it's just it's kitchen day. Eileen, bring in yon rocking chair for Henry. Poppet, shake him up a cushion. Anne – mind your head now, Henry, on the clothes airer. It's been good blanket weather this week, in and out of showers. When we daren't risk hay I wash blankets, but they tend to hang about and the ceiling's low. This is Grandpa."

Grandpa Hewitson turned his old head.

"It's an honour, Sir," said Henry.

"It's William," said Old Hewitson, "William over again. He had the TB had William and something muscular the matter with him, too. Started with him hitting his finger with the chopper when he was hewing hawthorn sticks. He had his arm off int' end. But then, Jimmie Meccer'll have told you."

Henry said he had not seen Jimmie Metcalf for –

"Legs lasting out with Jimmie Meccer, I hear," said Old Hewitson. "Mind you, he rested them long enough. Sat in yon shed for fifteen years till he struck lucky with his kitchen table and got hisself sorted out."

"Unfortunately I have only met him – "

"We had his dog. It used to lie in the road day after day. Nice dog but not much go about him. It died seven or eight years back or you could of seen it and told him about it. You can see his cottage anyway. You'll like to see that. It's close by. Our Bell and his wife, Poppet, and their Anne live there."

"That," said Henry, "will be the old farmhouse, Light Trees?"

"No," said Grandpa and turned back to the fire. It might

have been that Henry had never existed. The room, for Grandpa Hewitson, had emptied of him.

"Light Trees is a hill farm away up above the quarries," said Mrs Teesdale. "It belongs to Grandpa. It's right away up the fell."

"It is Light Trees I came to England about," said Henry and he put every one of his fingers together and then his two thumbs and his elbows very precisely on the ends of the arms of the rocking chair. "My father once told me of Light Trees. Your daughter lives at Light Trees?"

Eileen said after a little pause that, no, she lived beyond, in the only farm beyond. It was her husband's own farm and grand low-lying land. Dark Trees. No, they didn't own Light Trees.

"And you live here with your daughter, Mr Hewitson?"

"Yes, he lives here with us," said Mrs Teesdale since Grandpa Hewitson was closely examining the coals. "He's lived here since long since. Ever since Mother died. He does own Light Trees, though."

"So Light Trees stands empty?"

"Light Trees," said Mrs Teesdale – while Eileen and Poppet and Poppet's Anne stood still – "is let. It's been let over twenty years. To the same family."

"To a local family I take that to be?"

"No. No. Friends. Old friends."

"Not members of our family then? My family said that the house – there is a tradition that the house was never to pass out of the family and often passed to cousins?"

"It hasn't passed out of the family," said Poppet. "It's Grandpa's. He lets it. To London folk. They've taken good care of it. It was a bonny mess when they took it on by all accounts. They've been coming up here a thousand years."

"They will be sorry to leave it," said Henry. "It would be bad luck I understand for it to pass out of the family. I remember my father saying this. It's an old tradition."

131

Poppet suddenly thumped down a pot of rum-butter she was holding and crashed out of the room. Her temper was still uncertain.

"I remember distinctly my father saying that the one who should rightly inherit Light Trees would be me. Over the years I seem to have remembered it more clearly. Before I came away from South America I looked it up in his papers and it is all written down. The deeds of Light Trees. Here they are," and he took from his expensive slithery briefcase an old piece of paper and laid it on the stool on top of Old Hewitson's feet.

Then he left – to walk the Quarry Hill to survey the property to be left to him when Grandpa Hewitson died.

I am Anne Teesdale. I am the daughter of Bell and Poppet Teesdale. I am eleven and shall marry Harry Bateman who is a friend of my father, though much younger, he is a friend of all our family. He does not know that I shall marry him, nor does anybody else except perhaps my grandfather Hewitson and nobody knows exactly what my grandpa knows or doesn't know because he's about ninety years old.

Harry Bateman is the most beautiful, glorious, peaceful man and he lives in London but really belongs up here where he's been visiting since he was a baby. Here is the ancient kingdom of Cumbria and our part is the Hollow Land which is where I was born and have never left except when they sent me to a boarding school. I came back before the Crisis and I shan't leave again.

This place was the home of Eric Bloodaxe the Viking, The Lord of the Marches of Harcla, the Headless Horsewoman of Stainmore, the Hand of Glory, Granny Crack the Loony and my grandfather who is almost in folklore already. It was not the home of my mother Poppet, but you'd never guess. She came here about my age, my mother, on holiday with my important grandmother who is a household word. We never see her. My mother Poppet, decided to marry my father the day she met him. Harry will settle here for good too when he can afford to – say six years from now when I marry him and he'll not fret for other places neither. It's that sort of a place, the Hollow Land and he's that sort of a man.

But it isn't easy to get a footing here.

Just wait.

This is the account of the two most eventful days of my life to date. They ended this evening and must be recorded at once before I go to sleep, in case the slenderest detail should be lost to the world.

Harry was to come on the steam train from London yesterday morning. He'd booked the ticket months ago, as you have to with only one train a day, and Bell (my father) and I were up at dawn with the dew soaking white on the fields outside the kitchen window, white ash in the fire grate and nobody stirring, not even the five yellow cats asleep on chairs. My father opens the back door and slings the cats out in the yard one by one. He can't bide cats, he says, though they come trying to sit all over him. We drink each a cup of tea and I'm hoppitty skippety mad round the place because of Harry coming.

"Give over," he says, Dad, while I'm dancing and flapping toast about. "You'll wake your mother," and I notice he's right gruff.

Just standing, he is, staring out at the fields with the sun ready to come up over them, turning the four big oaks black and throwing spars and bars of dazzle across the lane and up towards Quarry Hill. You can't see any fells from down here. It's alongside my Granny Teesdale's farm house, this one, a little old house once lived in by some fat American with no legs called Jimmie Meccer. I never worked out who he was but he found some magic bit of furniture or pot of gold or some such and away he went and married a millionaire.

133

Anyway, we got his little house with its shed and it's grand.

Behind it there's a stable, old as Henry the Eighth with a little trap in it as old as Henry the Eighth's grandfather but a godsend since the Crisis. When the oil dried up and we all had to think again, my father, Bell, burrowed about in the stables and came out with this old trap, called a digby. It needed new springs, which Harry made last year – "He can do owt," my dad says – and it needed new seats which my gran Teesdale made out of old patch quilts, and new wheel-spokes which Harry went passionate over and painted reds and blues and yellows like the gypsies, said he, though gypsies seem to me always just to be sat by the road in old tin cans. Since the Crisis the gypsies have no colour in them. They mend old petrol tins and sit by the roadside watching you, and then move on. They're still good at finding horses. They've not left one wild now, though Harry says that there would be many a dozen ponies all over Wateryat Bottom when he was my age, dropping big fat foals that never knew saddle or bridle and lived and died free.

Well –

Away we're to go to Oxnumb station, Dad and I, to pick up the steam train and Harry off it. It's the best day of the year, the first day of Harry's holidays, the day he says he comes to life on, the day he comes back to Light Trees, the farm house that has been his real home since he was four or five year old; that you feel was Batemans always, even before the Romans.

"*Git* over," swears my dad, Bell, at the pony. He thumps down the little digby shafts either sides of the pony's round fat tum – not so round as once for the pony gets plenty exercise these days, though he doesn't often get so far as Oxnumb which is twenty miles.

And oh, the lovely ride in the sunrise through the village down Jingling Lane and over Coffin Bridge ("Why's it Coffin Bridge, Harry?" I used to ask when I was young. "Well because it caught a cold being so long with its feet wet. You can hear it coffin all night." Harry makes *wonderful* jokes) and along and along under the wild roses blowing, tangled over us ten feet high since we can't get any machinery to them now. And up the Midland Hill.

Then we turn left and the round low hills of Sedbergh stand ahead. "Old as the moon," said Harry, "but softer." So old that all the edges has been washed and rounded away, and the turf like velvet all to their tops. The sun's well up now and I never saw such a morning. Coming up to Cautley Spout the waterfall's hanging like a white thread far down the end of the dale – and closer in there's a red fox running in the bracken and looking quick and angry at all the hen houses still shut up in the yard of old Hannah's white farm where she went when her husband, Tatton, got over-excited living in a signal box when trains came back. (But he's well looked after now.)

Hannah's kitchen window is steamed over, so she's up. There's a spire of blue smoke going up from her chimney – a blue thread going up like the white waterfall coming down. And then I see two red squirrels. Two! They seem to be coming back since the traffic went. "Oh Dad," say I, "oh Dad!" – because of the red fox and the red squirrels and the white water and the blue smoke and the pale soft morning hills and the dew glittering on the grass poking up all down the middle of the broken tarmac road. "Oh Dad – it's grand!"

He just sits there looking at nothing at all except the backside of the pony.

"Dad?"

"Uh?"

"Dad – it's *grand*. It's a grand day. Isn't it?"

"Aye," and he gives the most terrible great sigh. A sigh to end the world.

"What's up then?"

"Not owt."

"Well, summat's up."

"Some*thing*." (He goes on about words though civilisations fall. I have to use different words from his, don't ask me why.)

"What is?"

"Nowt."

We clip-clop on. Now and then the pony, who's feeling happy as I am, gives a great blow down his nose and twirls its tail around.

"*Give* over," says Dad like thunder.

Our little daft dog – Border terrier – looks like a scrubbing brush. When it dies, Harry says, we'll nail a board to his back and *use* him for a scrubbing brush. This dog, Kipper, it starts walking out along the digby shaft. Dad doesn't see it at first. It goes tippety-tappitty, tappy-lappy along the shaft till it gets right up against the pony's ear. Then it sits down to have a quiet chat just as Dad sees it.

"GIVE over!" he bellows. So Kipper falls off.

We have to stop and me get down and go and scrape it out of a ditch where it's weeping and carrying on and pretending its back legs is done for. I'm nearly dying laughing – as Dad would be normally – and I drop it back in the digby and climb up beside it – and a minute later it's walking up alongside the pony's ears again.

"Dad," I say, "what is it? What's up? You're right twined."

"Stop talking so broad."

"Well you're miserable. What is it? Harry's coming. Come on – *Harry's* coming."

"Aye, I know," he says, "it's nowt. Just something I have to tell him. Don't tek on now. It'll be right, I dare say. In time."

I've never known him low like this – and quiet. We go clopping past the dew pond with the starey-eyed house behind it, past the queer old farm with the long Quaker windows, on and on through Sedbergh and away the other side. At last we get to the bridge that crosses the old motorway, and we stop to give the pony a rest, and we get down, hoping maybe to see a car go by.

It's cracking already, the old road, and the white lines nearly worn away. The verges are like flower shows – every wild flower you can think of tossing about now there's no fumes or cutters to keep them away. It's a disaster of course but it's funny how it seems usual now. Down what they used to call the central reservation there are some fair-sized trees and shabby great clumps of pink willow-herb. Down the tarmac the carriage way is being forced open in a long crack like in chocolate cake when you bend it over too tight, when you're making a Swiss roll. And out of the crack's coming bright green grass and white daisies.

"It'll look like a Roman road soon," I say. "Antique."

"Oh – it'll not come to that. Give it time. It's just till they get things sorted out. It's had its advantages, the Crisis. Look – here's a car coming."

We watch the solitary little electric car coming bashfully along the great motorway at about 30 m.p.h. all the big daisies nodding at it. I run to the other side of the bridge and watch it disappearing for miles, clicking away to the horizon and the long rocks near Penrith.

"They'll be walking the geese and the cattle along here soon," I said, "like in the Middle Ages."

Dad goes back to silence.

"Harry says in the Middle Ages the cattle used to wear special little shoes on the hard roads to stop their hooves wearing out. And the poor geese had their feet dipped in hot tar."

Dad's not listening.

"First in hot tar and then in sand and then in hot tar again. Awful, Harry said."

"It'll not come to that," said Dad, "Come on – we'll miss the train."

There's such a crowd on Oxnumb platform it looks like the old films of the War long long ago and I'm afraid, all of a sudden, I'll miss Harry. Especially as Dad, who's tall, wouldn't come on the platform with me to see over heads. He's still standing dumb in the station yard with the dog and the digby. For a minute in the hubbub – for it's standing room and hanging-out-of-doors-room in the trains now – James, Harry's brother who's travelled a lot as a Geologist, says it's like India here now – I think, he's not come. He's not managed it. They didn't keep his seat. He'll never get another ticket. He's stuck in London till next Spring.

Then there he is.

Harry.

A bicycle under one arm, a haversack on his back and his lovely, untroubled face. And I rush and I cling and I hug him.

"We're int' yard. Dad's int' yard with the cart. I came on."

"Now then, Anne."

"Oh, Harry!"

"Now then. We're all set up. Now then."

His voice is London but it'll start changing by the time we reach Sedbergh. He'll be talking like Dad by time we reach the Midland Hill.

"Now then," says Harry as he sees Dad.

"Now then," says Dad with one of his nods – but not with his usual brightening up of eyes.

We clop off.

"Something amiss then?" Harry looks down as we cross the motorway bridge. "By, but the flowers! Look at them cracks."

"It's not for ever," says Dad. "No good getting moped.

A crisis gets over. It's meant remarkable little change and much more labour to be got for farmers. Things'll change. They must. We're not that near finished."

"Aye, they'll change. They do," said Harry, taking the dog on his knee, " and there again they don't." He began to hum one of his tunes. He's not got much of a voice, Harry.

Usually Dad starts groaning when Harry sings. "Well you've not changed," or "Put the cat out someone," or "This is where we all start suffering," etc. But today Harry drones on and Dad seems not to hear him. It quite puts Harry off.

When we pass Hannah's house – the fox has gone and the chickens are out round her feet like autumn leaves and the blue smoke not noticeable now – we see her pinning up her washing on a line. Two sheets, two pillow-cases, like squares of snow that lie all year at the top of Skidder mountain. I see Harry look away over at Hannah and think Hannah's washing looks like squares of snow that lie all year on Skidder mountain. His thoughts are my thoughts quite often.

"Now then," Hannah calls and we see her wave both arms and nod her head up and down far away, and her voice comes over to us a second later. "Now then, young Harry."

At top of the Midland Hill the day's getting on and we're in sight of home – or rather Harry's home which is Light Trees. You can just see it if you know where to look. First find the quarry, pale orange and white, then keep your eyes moving upwards and left a bit. Now then, up and left again beyond the top field – and there's Light Trees with its white end wall: and in an arc around it the bright green of the Home Field in the middle of the brown fell, like its halo.

Dad stops the cart and Harry looks.

"Hay in then?" he says.

"Just about."

"In off the Home Field. Grand green fog growing."

"Aye. There's still some hay to get off Miners' Acre."

"Aye, I can see. And there's still some not cut by the looks

139

of over Tailrigg. What's all them dinosaurs standing about in Wharton Hall? Didn't know we'd gone that far back."

Dad laughs – at last! – "Three old balers broken down together. No proper oil. Well – scything's only thing now and pitchforks if you can teach how."

"Your grandad out pitchforking then?"

(This is a joke because as I said Grandpa Hewitson is cruising around towards a hundred years old.)

"Quarry's improved in looks," says Harry, letting his eye go lower again. "Trees is coming back. Hanging gardens. It'll be back to Granny Crack's days next."

"As long as it's not back to Granny Crack," says my father. And I feel much much better. Even a feeble joke like this is better than the long, terrible unhappy silence. What's more Bell, my father, seems to have given himself a shake and his mouth gone sensible again.

"Anne," he says, "jump out lass. We'll walk the horse down the hill. Stop back, and Harry and I'll take his bridle. The surface is bad and he'll slither hisself down else."

"Wait on," says Harry, still staring far away over at Light Trees, "there's folks in the Home Field. Men. Four of them."

"Walk on down, Anne," says Dad. "Go on. Walk on now. We'll catch you."

I don't. I climb the hedge-side just behind them and start picking meadowsweet and vetches and as they move down I move down behind them, but so as I can hear. They forget me.

"Four men standing about. Walking about. Look you there now, Bell – they've got posts in their hands. I'll have to get shot of them. They'll ruin the fog. Who's let 'em go marching about yonder?"

"Harry – " says Dad. There's a terrible pause.

Then quiet and steady and simple, as Dad is, he tells this most awful thing.

This man, this queer South American man as came lately all smooth in a pale suit with a pale face with pale eyes like a sheep with fluke and sloped-down, drippy shoulders – he has come to take Light Trees away from Harry.

All these years and years Harry's family has rented Light Trees from us, since he was a baby, and thought it to be theirs forever – for who of us would want a house so high to farm (save me)? And so did we think it theirs. Yet all this time it has really been just waiting for this South American. It's to be his because he is a Hewitson and long ago someone with some sort of say in the matter wrote down that it was always to be owned inside our family. It's for this man to do as he pleases with – all long ago arranged.

For a long time – the time it takes to go weaving down the Midland Hill holding the bridle of a tired and slipping horse at the end of a long journey – Harry never spoke.

Then he said "I'd think it'd be of little use to him? Light Trees? He'll not have need of it. He's rich then?"

"He's rich – he drives a car. He'll not have need of it. It will be no use to him."

"Then he'll go on letting, as you have done?"

"He'll not let."

At the hill bottom on Coffin Bridge they climb in the digby, but Dad doesn't move off. The water goes tearing by below them, talking its head off, amber and slate and foamy white over the half-sunk backs of the rounded stones. I still stand to the side behind them.

"He'll not let the farm any more, Harry. He's no need for Light Trees but as soon as Grandad's dead he wants it. For his fancy. He's retired from work. He says things are going to start moving again here soon. Seems he's been to do with mining."

"With mining?" There's fright now in Harry – real fear and fright.

Steady as the stones below, my dad says, "He thinks

there's ores up there. Ores still worth a fortune. The lead and the silver, he says, was never worked out. They're ahead of us, since the Crisis, with engineering. He talks even of oil up there in the Hollow Land."

Then my, but I feel thrilled! For Harry, who's so gentle and sweet some folks call him almost daft sometimes, he gives himself a shake and says, "Come here now then, Bell, and gi's them reins and let's get on. Oil there may be and silver and lead there may be but he's not looking for it now. At present he's no more right in the Home Field than passing campers. And even campers asks permission. Did he ask permission?"

Dad looks a bit bewildered. "No – "

"Because he's family? He doesn't have to ask permission to go in my field because he's family? Seems to me I remember that terms of our lease was that the field is ours except for what hay you take off it. I may not be your family, Bell Teesdale, but my family's Light Trees' tenants and he's trespassing on my tenancy and he can get hisself off."

We go clattering and thundering like the hordes of the Celts and the Visigoths and when Gran and Mum come out to greet Harry when they hear us, their smiles turn into round surprises as we fly past. I've hitched myself up in the back with the bike and the haversack again now. I try to call back to them what's up and wave my arms and point up Quarry Hill, but Harry shouts, "Sit *still* will you? Sit down there, Anne, and keep your mouth shut."

I'm so surprised I thump down in the bottom of the digby floor on top of Kipper who gives a scream.

"Keep that damn dog quiet," bellows Harry and round the bend of Quarry Hill we go with Dad holding his old hat and the pony with its eyes rolling as if its heart won't last five more minutes. Then it gives a scream, too, because under the old red bridge on Quarry Hill – the place where Kendal's always on about the skeleton of a prehistoric woman and her prehistoric baby – probably they were run over when you come to think of it – comes this great wonderful, smoothly-running silvery electric car with the South American driving it and three men in town clothes in the back and nobody smiling. He pulls up not four feet from our digby.

"Reverse," yells Harry at them.

Toot, toot, toot, goes the South American.

"Get yon car sided by," bawls Harry. "Get on. Get ower there int' bank. Git ower."

The South American gets out of the car and makes to stroll towards us.

"I said OWER," said Harry, "git ower. You been in my field. I seed you from Midland Hill. Ruining the fog. Trampling the ground. Trespassing."

"I guess I can't trespass on what's to be my own."

"I guess you can," says Harry and grabs the horse whip.

Henry Roberto Hewitson III, or whatever he's called, steps back in to his car, locks the doors and winds up the windows. Harry pulls our pony over to the side and points down the hill. "Git going. Keep away. We've still got a police force and lawyers in this struggling country."

Then he turns to Dad. "And you get home an' all," he says, and he flings the horse whip back in the cart and he starts up to Light Trees on foot by himself.

Dad sits there.

The pony's got foam at his mouth and a drooping head and the dog's jumped out and disappeared. Dad just sits – on the dangerous bend. Just sits.

After a bit I pick up the flowers and haversack and lift down the bicycle and I look at Dad for a bit. Then I go on up Quarry Hill after Harry.

And the next day – this morning – there is an eclipse of the sun. I don't mean that Harry caused it and I don't mean that it was unexpected. Harry tells me it was known to be on the way by someone good at calculations several thousand years ago. "Goodness," said this astronomer, "what do you think? August 11th 1999 at eleven o'clock allowing for British Summer Time, ten if you call it G.M.T., there's to be a total eclipse of the sun in Cornwall where the Phoenicians live. They'll make a great fuss of it all over that cold changeable country where the wild folks are."

That is the way Harry spoke of it anyhow last time he was here. He makes things seem very alive. We have all been looking forward very much to this eclipse. If Harry hadn't been coming up here I would somehow, somehow have got to Cornwall where there'll be the real dramatics – the flames streaking out on either side of the black disc on the sun, the luminous haze for miles beyond, like spying at heaven. And the stars will come out in broad daylight. In Ancient Greece, Harry said, you got executed if anyone heard you say that an eclipse of the sun was due to natural causes. In China even today, Harry says, some folk think that an eclipse of the sun is when a serpent comes eating it up. In the South Sea Islands, Harry says, they think an eclipse is the sun and the moon making love with each other and all the stars are their children.

"Eclipse of the sun today," I say to Harry. I am up at Light Trees washing up his breakfast things and making his bed and seeing to the flowers I flung in a jug quick yesterday before he threw me out, wanting to be alone. "'Today's Arrangements – Total Eclipse of the Sun'."

"What's that?"

"What you told me about last time. How it said in *The Times* newspaper, 'Today's Arrangement – a total eclipse of the sun.' It must have been good to get a newspaper every day. And feel we were in charge of arrangements."

He said nothing.

"*Eclipse*, Harry," I said. "It's the eclipse. When do we start up?"

144

"Up?"

"Start up the Nine Standards. They'll all be there. The whole village and more. It'll be good. We're taking picnics I think."

"*All* be going?"

"Well, of course all. All the village, like for the Jubilee. Hannah's getting over from Cautley Spout. And they're pushing up the old Egg Witch. And there's to be Eileen's lot and our lot and Gran and Grandad – not Great Grandad of course – but almost everyone. That old farmer from Castledale that rescued you from the gypsies, and the South American. And Kipper. Not the cats though. Cats can get fuddled at an eclipse, Great Grandad says."

"I can get fuddled," said Harry. He went out in to the yard to see the old horse-rake he's doing up bit by bit, for it's quite a treasure now.

But when I look, he's just standing there beside it with a frown on his face. Such a sad look as you never saw. He's lost all the grand ferocity of yesterday now. He's just standing like an orphan.

And I think, however in all the world could Dad and Grandad and Great Grandad do it? Just because this Hewitson's a Hewitson. And just because of a scant bit of paper – not even a legal document, says my mother, Poppet (I heard her last night going for Dad like a serpent eating up the moon), just a sloppy bit of sentimental paper. And because there's money in it. Because this South American's offered shares to all of us in all he digs out, because times are hard and farmers cannot in the end resist money. "Harry can have a share, too," says my dad. "He'll need compensation – there being no other houses now to rent, all being bought up when the war scare was on in '84. This chap thinks there's a fair sized seam up above the bouse."

"Well we know there's a fair sized seam," said my mum. "We played as kids like Kendal showed us. We took the

145

bronze rods or even just the blackthorn twigs until they
twitched. And they did twitch, didn't they? Until what?
Until when? Until we put a nugget of ore in our pockets and
then they stopped because of the same ore underfoot."

My dad clattered about – I was listening up in my bed,
through the floor.

"Aye," says Mum, "and where did the seam come thickest? Where did Kendal say the real stuff lay? Underneath –
right underneath Light Trees long room, didn't it? It'll mean
taking Light Trees right down to the ground."

Watching Harry now I wonder if he's thought of this, too.
If he remembers playing looking for the seam. And I pray he
doesn't. He comes up the yard, back in to the porch.

I say, "Look, Harry, Great Grandad owns Light Trees. It
can't pass from him till he's dead. Nothing's going to happen
just yet anyway. Oh *Harry*!"

He glares.

"I know he's old – well very, very, old. But nothing's
changed yet, has it? Can you see Great Grandad letting them
dig up the Home Field? Putting great machines over Hartley
Birket? Wheels and trucks and that? Neither would Dad – I
know he wouldn't. Mum wouldn't let him."

"And pull down Light Trees' house itself," says Harry.
(So he knew.) "We always said when we were kids, Anne,
that the best of the seam runs just about where your feet
stand now."

I look down at my feet and think of the miserable old
chunks of lead or silver, maybe even the thick gummy pools
of oil right deeper in the dark, under the stone floor and the
earth and the limestone, below.

"They'd never," I say.

"Times are bad," says Harry. "The money's needed. This
house isn't needed. After all, I've got a roof of sorts over my
head in London. Where I was born. I've more than most.
We've been more than lucky, our family, having Light Trees

to come to for all these years. We always knew we didn't own it. Maybe it's time to start siding all by now. Maybe people should stay where they were first put."

"You great daft thing," say I, "Harry Bateman! What sort of a world would this be if people had stayed where they was born? What sort of a country this? There'd have been no Vikings bringing bees and honey and no Christians bringing Jesus Christ and no Celts with bronze and jewels and no Romans fixing up roads and laws and no Saxons with books and painting and lovely clothes and no new ideas from nowhere. No gypsies for excitement, all the way from India. No Italian prisoners Grandad talks about in the Last War bringing songs and that and no Chinese like over in Appleby cooking new food. This is what you've always told me, Harry Bateman. I wouldn't be here if my mum hadn't settled on marrying Bell first time she came up here at eleven."

"Some bad things wouldn't have got here neither," Harry said, but he came over and pulled my hair. "Sorry, old Anne. It'll all sort out likely."

Out of the window it wasn't exactly getting dark but the light was growing odd – slightly sombre.

"Hey, Harry," says I. "Look. It's starting. The eclipse of the sun. Come on. You're coming up, aren't you? Come on quick. You'll miss it. They'll be all up there at the Nine Standards ahead of us."

"All right then. I'm coming." He gives a sigh, but he looks better.

We set off together away over the fell, up Hartley Birket to the fell gate. We climb it and away over the marshy place that in twenty years Harry says nobody's remembered to take planks to throw across. We sog and we sough in the mud of the bogs – and we notice the colour of them is turning purplish. Reaching the first rise by the sheepfolds the stones of the walls are turning purplish, too. Away over, all the colours to Helvellyn, west, to Hell Beck, north, to Tailrigg, south have all gone wrong. It's like a television when someone's turned the colour down too far. My inside lurches about. Harry laughs. We look all round and at each other's face.

"You've turned bronzy," says Harry.

We go on up, and on up. Soon we can see the Standards, leaning forwards like Roman standards on the march, but when you get nearer they're fat as fir cones, black and huge like gigantic sheep droppings. Queer things at any time, standing there for all the earth and heavens to see and nobody knowing what they are. I wouldn't camp up here at night not for silver or gold or oil or even Harry.

Some folks say the Standards move about. You look for them and they're not there. You look again and they're about half a mile from where they ought to be – but I don't believe that, for they've always stood still for me.

You can wish for things on the Standards, but you should be careful, old Kendal says. Funny things went on up there once, he says. You have to be very sure you know what you're asking, wishing on the Standards.

The Standards crown the Rigg and over the gold sprays of the grasses and the peat hags and the scatters of rocks sit people who have come to see the eclipse of the sun. I can make out our family from here. They are busy with their picnics, all littered about – Hewitsons and Teesdales sitting a bit apart. Being the oldest sheep families they seem always a bit apart and more important.

It's darkening now and Harry and I sit down near the rest. There's silly shrieks and giggles here and there from kids, and "OOOH I'm frightened," and "Maybe it'll be end oft' world." Someone says, "We'd look right soft if it didn't happen."

"It'll happen all right," says someone. "It's happening. It's beginning."

"Hello, Harry," says Bell, my dad. He gives a stiff nod.
"Morning, Bell," says Harry, not looking at him.

Now all the peaks of Dufton, their tops caught up like tents, have turned black. And it's queer. It's as if there's darkness above and light below. It's like the light when the Helm Wind is blowing, but it's not bitter cold like when the Helm blows. The Helm can freeze you so that the old miners had to have their clothes cut off with knives. There's no wind here. Just the queer light that's not darkness nor shadow nor twilight.

People start saying that they can see the stars shining. And the birds have stopped singing, says someone. No curlews nor larks. Listen how quiet!

I listen. And I watch. Harry beside me. Even with an eclipse of the sun I can't forget this awful thing that's happened to Harry. And as the whole world grows darker and the colours die out of the light I lean back and touch the great rough stone Standard, leaning my back on it. Then I stretch up and press my hands in to the sharp hurting edges of the stones. "Keep Harry here," I pray, "keep him here."

And in the silence and the shadows – everyone has stopped talking, even whispering – there's the weirdest thing. There's the sound of a car. It comes from far, far away, then up nearer, up nearer and then it stops.

Then – no sign of lights. It must be over a fold – it starts again, and grows loud for a minute and then fainter and fainter still. And then it's far away again so that you have to strain to hear it at all.

As the car engine gets fainter the light begins to grow stronger. Soon you can make out true colours again. The tent-like mountains over Dufton are no longer black but purple and then blue. The Saddleback is lavender and the Sedbergh hills are getting back their plushy yellow haze. And so is the fellside, and the grass and stones we sit on, sweeping down to the old turf track, smooth and ancient with a thousand years of sheep. The grass grows honest, ordinary green again.

And standing on the track, all by himself and humped like a goblin and eating a piece of cake is my great grandad, Old Hewitson.

Everyone rushes at him.

Going on a hundred years old they all shout! Never been farther than the rhubarb patch in ten years. "Thirteen hundred feet up?" and we're all shouting and carrying on.

"You'll get your death!"

"You silly old man."

"However d'you get here?"

We run down and look him over and we fling clothes over him and he finishes his cake and starts laughing.

"Well, I missed it int' end," he says, "I tellt' him to get a move on but yon big motors are no good nowadays. I'll be glad to go back in the digby."

"Whatever? Why ever?"

"Well, yon poor little white thing from Brazil or wherever we were having a talk at home, and it suddenly took my fancy to come up to the Standards again. Just to give him something to do. To take his mind from his disappointment."

"Whatever's that?"

"Henry Hewitson's disappointment. About not being able to pull down Light Trees, poor little feller. He's gone now. He won't be back. He's gone back to South America."

Harry sat down on a rock. We all waited.

"Grandad," said Bell, "what's this then?"

"Well, he was talking on about silver and gold and the Crown Jewels and that that he says is buried under Light Trees flagstones and I said I'd not think there'd ever be much chance to find out.

"He says, 'When it's mine. After your day, Sir – '

"I says, 'And why is to be thine after my day?'

" 'Well,' he says, citing his piece of paper, 'I'm a Hewitson,' he says. 'All your lot has their farms and properties. Light Trees is for me and blood is thicker than water.'

"And I says that I never cared for that expression. Not in the very least. In fact I've always had more of a fancy to water – though mind I'm not a vegetarian."

"Will you get on, Grandad," roars my dad, Bell. My mother, Poppet, puts both her fists in her mouth and I daren't – I just daren't – look at Harry.

" 'Well,' says I, 'There's this Harry. He once went chasing after water when he was a bairn knee high and he gathered a bundle of it and when he gets it home it's all gone. And there's my lad's lad, Bell, nearly dies of bronchitis chasing water, too. But feeling it was worth it in the end. I've never been far from water all my life – though mind you I think nothing of the sea; I wouldn't thank you for it – there's seldom been a day I haven't heard the water running in the hollows of the fell. Yet every day has been different'."

"*Get* on, will you!"

" 'Well,' says I, 'your bit of paper's nowt. I've had it looked at by the solicitors when you were all up hay-making and pacing fields for treasure last week. There's a later bit of paper – mine. I wrote it out long since when Harry Bateman were thirteen year old and the little lass Anne just born. I left Light Trees to the little lass Anne, but Harry Bateman to be tenant for his life.' The solicitors said Henry Hewitson's bit of paper couldn't touch mine. It wasn't a patch on it."

"Mind you," he added, as everyone started humping him in to the digby and wrapping him in things, "I'se far from dead yet and I'll be wanting rent from Batemans until."

When the digby had gone on down – full up with Teesdales and Hewitsons and a trail of hangers-on behind, Harry and Bell and I stood watching the procession down the Nine Standards Rigg. It was a good sight – the little coloured cart and all the heads nodding and the talk and the exclamations and the running people in front and behind. Auntie Eileen had her latest new baby asleep on her arm, and there was the old Egg Witch like Boadicea in her pram, and my mother, Poppet, talking her head off, very decisive as usual and everyone I loved the most. I just wished Kendal was here back from the total eclipse in Cornwall – it couldn't have been better than here – and a few more Batemans.

But they will all be coming next week, even James from far away. And if we book the call in, we can telephone them. Telephone them to tell them not to worry about anything. Not ever again. For they are safe here for ever in the Hollow Land.

I was last down to the fell gate, feeling quite dizzy and a bit sickish and not that keen to turn and look round at the Standards. I could feel them looking down at me, boring their old magics in to my back. So I walked on steady to the fell gate.

Bell and Harry were messing with it, swinging the old thing to and fro.

"When things look up again," said Bell, "I'm getting an electronic sneck on this fell gate." They said not one word about Great Grandad Hewitson, or yesterday, or the South American or Light Trees at all.

"Beats me," says Dad, "how people still can't shut this fell gate. First one person leaves it open for others behind, then along come the stragglers and think that's how it's meant to be – and it's sheep in the meadows and cows on the fell."

"Folks don't change," says Harry. "Look, they've even taken off with the twine."

"I'll get some," shouts I. "There's John Robert twine in the Light Trees' clipping shed. Wait on."

And I go flying and leaping down Hartley Birket and over the wall into the Home Field. And here's Light Trees looking at me with its old and smiling face, quiet and untroubled in the green fell side.

BOOKS BY JANE GARDAM

BILGEWATER
THE HOLLOW LAND
(published by Greenwillow Books)

A FEW FAIR DAYS
A LONG WAY FROM VERONA
THE SUMMER AFTER THE FUNERAL
(published by Macmillan Publishing Co., Inc.)

BRIDGET AND WILLIAM
(published by Julia MacRae Books)

GOD ON THE ROCKS
THE PINEAPPLE BAY HOTEL
THE SIDMOUTH LETTERS
(published by William Morrow and Company, Inc.)

Jane Gardam was born on the northeast coast of Yorkshire and spent her childhood in Coatham, where her ancestors had lived since the eleventh century. Now married, with three children, and living in London, Jane Gardam regularly goes back to the North, and spends as much time as she can in the Cumbrian fells. Before her marriage, she was literary editor for *Time and Tide*; her career as a novelist began in 1971 with the publication of *A Few Fair Days*. Since then she has written four more children's books and three adult novels, one of which, *God on the Rocks*, was a nominee for the Booker Prize. She is a fellow of the Royal Society of Literature.

Jane Gardam has traveled extensively, and now finds she has invitations from as far afield as the United States and Australia to speak as one of the outstanding writers of today, hailed by critic Auberon Waugh as "head and shoulders above the normal run."